TOROPO:
TENTH WIFE

BY

Linda Harvey Kelley

A SEQUEL

The sequel to Toropo: Tenth Wife is now in writing
And will be titled Toropo's Sister: Tawa.
Look for it in Christian Bookshops.

THIS EDITION

This is the original version of Toropo: Tenth Wife,
as written by Linda Harvey Kelley,
Not the condensed, simplified version as published by
Heinemann, a Division of Reed International Books Australia Pty
Ltd for the Department of Education, PNG

Copyright by Linda Harvey Kelley 1995

ISBN: 978-1-934447-19-2

All rights reserved. No part of this publication may be
reproduced, stored in a retrieval system or transmitted in any
form or by any means whatsoever without the prior permission of
the copyright owner. Apply in writing to the publisher.

First published 1995
Second printing 1997
Third printing 2008

Cover and text design by Leigh Ashforth
Cover illustration by Evelinsa Frescura

First printing by Rigby Heinemann, Victoria, Australia

Third printing printed by
Whispering Pines Publishing
11013 Country Pines Road
Shoals, Indiana 47581, USA

Dedication

To all the girls in Papua New Guinea
facing the challenges portrayed here
and
In Memory of all the girls
who died facing these challenges

About the Author

Linda Harvey came to the Southern Highlands of Papua New Guinea with her missionary parents and brothers when she was thirteen years old. She married George Kelley Jr. at Katiloma, Kagua Sub-District, in 1970. Their first son was born in Mount Hagen Hospital, and they had two more children, a son and a daughter in the USA. Each child married and has two children making them six beloved grandchildren.

Linda has taught and/or counseled at the Muskegon River Youth Home, Pineview Homes, and Baker College of Cadillac, Michigan. She has also taught for shorter periods in Kiev, Ukraine, and longest of all in Papua New Guinea.

Foreword

The tragic story of Toropo, set just after Independence, makes us think about issues that are still important in today's Papua New Guinea.

Our Constitution states as its first National Goal that each person should be able to free himself or herself from "every form of domination or oppression," and to "develop as a whole person in relationship with others."

This is also Toropo's goal. The sufferings and injustices that come upon her remind us of the difficulties that we also face in trying to attain the freedom and development that our Constitution assures us is our right.

In Toropo's case, she suffers from an enforced marriage to a man she does not love; she suffers from horrific violence and from the constant threat of even greater violence.

Domestic violence is a form of oppression that is a worldwide problem, but each country suffers from it in its own way. In Papua New Guinea, domestic violence has both traditional and modern causes. In the story of Toropo, we see an extreme example of violence and oppression in a largely traditional setting; but we know that there are other Toropos around the country – in villages and towns, in cities and settlements – who are still struggling, two decades after Toropo's troubles, to win their basic constitutional right to freedom from oppression.

This novel, *Toropo: Tenth Wife*, tells a tragic story. When we finish reading it we should turn our attention to the real tragedies of violence and oppression – in our own homes, next door, or down the street.

Josepha Kanawi
Secretary, Law Reform Commission
Chairperson, Women and Law Committee

Glossary of Imbo-Ungu Words

ai!	hey!
ama	mother
ambo	woman
ambo kunana	love chant, head-turning (tanim het)
ambo mopene	beautiful young girl, debutante
aminienga glapa!	an exclamation (lit. "your mother's father!")
ango	brother, sibling of the same sex
ara	father
aya	sister
bagol	girl
balkangoma	children
konjo nowi	"eat-it-raw" – cucumber
ere!	exclamation *olaman!*
imbo	people, real, natural, real people
Imbo-Ungu	Real Talk, or Real People's Talk
iye	man
kambe ulke	isolation hut
kango	boy
kapogla	all right
kariyapa	mirror
keri	bad
kogol	dear little, tiny, (a term of endearment)
koinje	(bamboo) tongs
kondodle	red, red skins, light-skinned
Konopu	friend, dearest (lit. thought, part of the verb "to love")
Kuro Kelkawe	the good spirit
ltemo	it's evident, or on evidence
magol	son

moglowiyo	good-bye (lit. you may stay)
mundu	mound for planting *kaukau*
nagol	but
nanga	my, mine
owa!	exclamation (lit. dog!)
owiyo	you may come
paaimbo	truly
paa-tsingo-we	very delicious
pamili	let's go
Peyamo-peli	where the spirit Peyamo sleeps
puyo	good-bye (you may go)
tsingo-we	delicious, sweet
wenepo	young
wenopoma	teen-agers

Glossary of Pidgin Words

ai gris	"eye-grease," flirt
apinum	afternoon (a greeting)
bilum	net bag, or netting worn on the body
dia tumas	expensive, very dear
go nating	"go nothing," shack up with someone, without marriage ceremony or brideprice
haus-sik	"house-sick," hospital
kalabus	jail
kaukau	sweet potato
kiap	government officer
kunai	tall, sharp-edged grass (perhaps elephant grass)
laplap	length of cloth
lapun	old person

meri	woman, female
Mi go wokabaut gen nau.	I'm going to go wandering again now.
Mi no save.	I don't know.
mumu	pit oven in the earth
olaman	"all the men," an exclamation without literal meaning
pitpit	a cane, similar to bamboo but much thinner, smaller (though 6-8 feet tall)
purupuru	grass skirt
rausim	"rouse," send away, dismiss, discharge, take out or away
rabis meri	"rubbish woman," whore, prostitute
singsing	dance
toea	penny, cent
Tru tumas	Truth! or "That's very true!"
yo, -eyo -iyo	la, la, la, la, la, in singing (no translatable meaning)

CHAPTER ONE

Toropo heard the distant call of her best friend. She yodelled an answer. A few minutes later Keri came into view.

"*Konopu*, my friend, working hard?"

"Not too hard to talk to you at the same time. I'm so glad to see you!"

With a swish of her grass skirt Keri plopped down on the ground.

"You planning on working till late?"

"Not too late. I want to be home when Turi returns from school. Why? What's up?"

"Just wait until you hear! Joseph has a friend visiting him. He came yesterday afternoon. Ere! Is he handsome! You must come and see him just as soon as you can."

"Where's he from?"

"From the coast, same as Joseph. Only he's ever so much younger. Wait till you hear his Pidgin English. It sounds like jew's-harp music to your ears! He is the most dazzling fellow I have ever met!"

"True!? I guess I will have to see him, won't I? He sounds too good to miss. How long is he staying?"

"I haven't heard."

"Have you talked with him?"

"Not really. He did speak to me though. He was joking with the catechist and a bunch of us were laughing too. All of a sudden he looked straight at me and said, 'What's your name, Laughing Eyes?'"

"Did he really? Oh, Keri, how nice!"

"I didn't answer, of course. I just hid my face in my *laplap*, but Joseph told him."

Toropo continued to dig while she listened. Her capable hands were forming a perfectly rounded mound for the planting of sweet potatoes.

"Tell me more about him. What else did he say?"

Keri reached out and touched her friend's hair. "Oh, Toropo, I wish I had hair and skin like yours. How do you keep them so soft and lovely?"

"By washing, dearest, as I've told you before. I just had a swim in the Pawendo River yesterday."

"St-st-st. Naughty, naughty! 'You'll never catch a man with skin like a frog,'" quoted Keri.

"Nonsense! That's just a ridiculous old wives' tale invented to keep us girls busy in the gardens instead of playing in the water. Bani told me all the schoolgirls bathe and swim every day and none of them have skin like frogs. He even asked one of his teachers for me if girls' skin reacts any differently to water than boys' skin. His teacher said 'No.'"

"No matter how much I washed and combed my hair it would never look like yours though," sighed Keri, fingering her own wiry curls. "May I comb yours while you work?"

"*Kapogla.*"

Keri went to the nearby tree where Toropo's *bilum* and *laplap* were hanging. From the *bilum* she took the bamboo comb which Bani had made for his sister.

"Maybe he won't notice me if you're there," Keri worried, as she shaped Toropo's fluffy halo into a soft Afro.

"Why do you want me to go with you then?"

"Because you're my *Konopu*. And I want you to see this dazzling fellow who called me 'Laughing Eyes.' Will you quit soon and come with me?"

"Yes, if you do want me to. As soon as I finish these two mounds I'll dig some *kaukau* for tonight. *Ama* and my brothers are coming to see my garden soon after *big-sun*. We'll walk back with them."

An hour later they were showing *Ama* Toropo's garden. Toropo had her four-month-old baby brother in her arms. His warm, chubby body felt soft against her own. When she laid him down in her arms he immediately began nuzzling at her bare breast, his little red lips searching for the nipple.

"Oh, little *Konopu*! I have no milk for you." She cuddled him close and pointed out a patch of bush spinach to her mother.

"But your *eat-it-raw* (cucumbers) are what amaze me most, daughter. I have never seen any do better. Won't we enjoy serving them to our friends and relatives at the *singsing*?"

"Yes."

"And my little Debutante, if a man wants to show the brideprice for you, I ought to bring him here to see this garden. It should raise your price by at least three pigs!"

Toropo's eyes shone but a lump in her throat kept her from making any reply. All her life she had been alternately spurred on with the words, "If you do this you will bring us a good price," or threatened with the words, "You won't be worth two pigs if you can't do that!" Therefore her parents could not now give her any higher commendation on her striving than to tell her she would bring them a large bride price. This was the standard or goal set for every baby born of the female sex in the Southern Highlands of Papua New Guinea. And Toropo would accomplish it! Her mother had assured her she would.

"I'm going farther into the bush to get some bark for thread, Toropo. Can Teni stay with you?"

"*Kapogla, Ama,*" said Toropo taking her four-year-old brother's hand. "Keri and I are going home soon. She wants me to go with her to see a fellow who's visiting the catechist. Teni can go with us."

"*Kapogla* then, be good girls." *Ama's* eyes twinkled at her daughter as she took the baby from her.

Toropo ran quickly to her *bilum* of *kaukau*, *eat-it-raw*, and *pitpit* shoots. She folded her *laplap* and balanced it on her head. She knotted the long ends of the big *bilum* and swung it around, up, and onto her *laplap* in one swift movement. She had been practicing this act since she was three years old, starting, of course, with much lighter loads. She swung the second bag into place on top of the first and reached forward with one bare foot for her garden stick. Grasping it firmly between her big toe and second toe she lifted it to her hand as dexterously as if her foot had been a third hand.

"I'm ready," she called to Keri and Teni. "Let's go."

On the long walk home Toropo said little, concentrating on carrying her load up and down the steep hillsides and stepping carefully on the treacherous trail. Her bare feet sought out good grips in the slippery clay and on the single poles that bridged the mountain streams.

Toropo put her bags in the hut. The three of them hurried up the trail to the mountain spring. They cupped their hands under the bamboo water trough protruding from the bank, and splashed the water over their faces. Toropo and Teni drank long and thirstily. Toropo reshaped her crushed Afro and then wrapped her *laplap* around her body, bringing the two ends up to cross in front and tie behind her neck. It resembled a sunsuit, just covering her hips, with her *purupuru* flowing out beneath it.

"Why cover up?" asked Keri, eyeing her friend curiously.

"I wish I had a blouse," sighed Toropo. "I've been saving and I have almost enough money to buy one. I'd like to cover up all the time. The boys stare so anymore. And this fellow is from the coast, you say. Bani says everyone wears clothes on the coast. Even the small children."

The girls sauntered up the hill as they talked. The village of Tona consisted of ten huts, one grass church and the catechist's house. His house was made of bush materials also, but it was built on the Western style. It had windows to let in light, and a door one could enter standing erect. It was not wind proof like the low huts but the catechist's family could afford to buy blankets.

"Come and join the fun!" called Eleppe, as the girls drew near the group of young people. "Peter has been playing his guitar and singing for us. Come on, Peter, give us another song. Here are two more to add to your audience."

"*Tru tumas.* If it isn't Laughing Eyes herself!" exclaimed the young man. "And who is your friend?"

Ellepe answered for Keri, though it seemed Peter did not hear her for he was staring at Toropo as though he were bewitched.

Toropo allowed herself one glance into those admiring eyes before she quickly dropped her head.

"How long has he been singing?" she whispered to Ellepe as she sat down, wondering how much longer he would continue.

"Since *big-sun* actually, but nothing steady. He chats and jokes between songs. I wish I understood Pidgin better. I don't always catch everything he says."

Peter watched the two girls talking together in a language he could not understand. How could he make the little beauty look at him again? What striking eyes she had under those long, curly, thick lashes.

He strummed a chord and she looked up instantly. He began to sing.

Toropo's eyes never wandered from his face. She drank in the music, absorbing every note, submerging her very soul in it. He could sing! There was no doubt about that. Not that Toropo had heard enough singing to be a competent judge, but he sang better than anyone she had ever heard. So this was what a guitar looked like. Bani had described them and she had heard them on the catechist's radio. Two students at Kauapena had ukuleles, but what were they compared to a guitar?

Peter tried to glance briefly at each of the young faces before him but his eyes kept returning inadvertently to Toropo. He reveled in her beauty as obviously as she basked in his music. The song ended. Toropo returned to reality.

"Oh, don't stop," she begged.

How could any man resist such eloquent eyes? But he wanted to hear her talk.

"You liked my song?"

"Yes."

"Can you sing?"

"No."

"What song would you like me to sing?"

"I don't know the names of any songs. Please just sing anything."

What else could he say to keep her talking?

"Who taught you to speak Pidgin?"

"My brothers."

"Are they here?"

"No."

"Where are they?"

"At school."

"What school?"

"Bani is at Ialibu High School."

"And there is another?"

"Turi is at Kauapena Community School."

"Did you go to school?"

"No."

"Why not?"

"I don't want to talk. Please sing."

"In a little while. Talk to me first."

Toropo was silent and turned her face away from him.

"Laughing Eyes, do you speak Pidgin?"

"Yes," answered Keri.

"Then talk to me?"

"About what?"

"You three girls."

"What about us?"

"Do you come to church here?"

"Sometimes."

"Why not all the time?"

"*Mi no save.*"

"What else do you do?"

"*Mi no save.*"

"Aw, come on, talk to me?"

Keri hesitated a moment, then asked, "How long are you staying?"

"Who? Me?"

"Yes, you."

"In the Southern Highlands you mean?"

"I mean here, with Joseph."

"Oh. A few days, I guess."

"How many is that?"

"Maybe three. Maybe ten. Who knows?"

Keri withdrew into her *laplap* and said no more. So he was just passing through, was he? She might have known.

The girls chatted quietly among themselves for a few minutes. Toropo looked up at Peter.

"If you have finished singing, I'm going home."

"Oh, not so fast! You just got here! Why hurry off?"

No answer.

After a pause he strummed a few chords. Again Toropo was instantly attentive. He sang along this time without bothering to look around.

"Some day you'll hear me calling
   You'll hear me calling you,
Promise me you'll answer,
   Promise me true.

"Some day I'll stop my wandering
   Some day 'twill all be through.

Promise me you'll answer
When you hear me calling you.

"I wandered over mountains
I wandered through the vale,
I wandered through the weather,
Rain and storm and hail.

"I wandered o'er the country
I saw its every view.
Some day I'll stop my wand'ring,
I'll wander back to you.

"Some day you'll hear me calling
You'll hear me calling you.
Promise me you'll answer,
Promise me true."

 He strummed the last chord and Toropo sighed. With only short pauses between each song he sang several more in quick succession. Then he put up his guitar saying, "I can't sing any more."
 "Just as well," commented one young fellow in his audience. "The rain is coming up river there. We couldn't sit here much longer." Turning to the boy beside him he said, "Come on, I'll race you as far as your house." He nudged his friend in the ribs and they were off.
 Toropo and Teni rose. Toropo took a few steps towards Peter.
 "Thank you," she said softly. "Thank you for singing. It was … it was sweeter than a whole bush full of birdcalls."
 "I'd sing all night to you if I could," responded Peter eagerly.
 "Thank you," she whispered again, and taking Teni's hand in hers she moved gracefully down the trail.
 Peter's eyes followed her until she was out of sight.

CHAPTER TWO

"Guess what, Toropo?" Teni was tired of his sister's long silence.

"What's that, Pet?"

"I learned of another possum's nest not far from *Ama's* garden. I found it this morning. I saw its tracks and I followed them straight to its home. I didn't tell any of the boys or their big brothers would get it. I can't wait till Turi gets here. He'll help me catch it and we'll eat it together. *Tsingo-we!*"

"Good for you, Bright Eyes. I'm anxious for Turi to come too."

"I suppose you want him to teach you something new?" asked *Ama*.

"Of course," grinned her daughter as she picked up another *kaukau* to peel with her bamboo peeler.

"You've already learned Pidgin. Why do you want to learn English too?"

"Because the boys are learning English. Because there are no books in Pidgin. The books Turi and Bani show me are all in English. And ... oh, I don't know. Just because I want to keep on learning and learning."

"You are learning lots more important things. These *eat-it-raw* are juicy and delicious."

An hour later *Ara* (father) was there and they were withdrawing the baked *kaukau* from the ashes.

"Where could that boy be?" fumed *Ara*. "He must have got a late start," soothed *Ama*.

"But I told him once long ago to always come straight home."

"Maybe they had some special activities at school and didn't get out as early as usual," suggested Toropo.

"Yes, it is well that you made two torches, daughter," said Bossboy Pombo glancing at the two long bundles of dried *pitpit* cane placed near the wall. "One wouldn't be enough if I have to go far. I'll leave as soon as I've eaten. No use going on an empty stomach when I don't know how far I may have to go." As *Ara* spoke he slapped the ashes from another *kaukau* and took a huge bite.

"I'll go with you," said Toropo.

"So will I," piped Teni.

"If Torombaiyo's house wasn't beside the trail, I wouldn't be nearly so worried."

"Who is Torombaiyo?" asked Teni.

"He's a man from the Imi tribe who used to live down-river from Kauapena, but he moved up-river a couple years ago. When I was a boy my uncle killed a woman from the Imi tribe as a payback for another killing years earlier."

"I think they've forgotten by now."

"Never forget, son! Never forget a grievance. Your enemies won't and that's certain! You must pay back every wrong even if you have to wait till you're an old man to do it."

"But how will Tomtom ..."

"Torombaiyo," prompted his father.

"How will Torombaiyo know who Turi is?"

"He may well have made it his business to find out. If you have an enemy, son, it's your duty to learn every detail about that man and his family."

Teni silently stared into the fire, thinking it all over.

Bossboy Pombo studied his little son proudly. What other man had a son, newly weaned, who asked such intelligent questions? What other youngster fresh from his mother's breast was ready to learn the tactics of revenge? The payback was one of the most important traditions, and it was well to teach a boy all about it as early as possible. Pombo wondered if already Teni might be applying his newly learned wisdom to some small grievance with a playmate. That was undoubtedly the way to begin.

The Big-Man's thoughts followed a trail they had often run before. One of my sons will be able to take my place as a leader when I am too old to lead my tribe any longer. If Bani and Turi get too absorbed in education and never return from the white man's world, then it may be Teni here. Of course there are Yapa and Yombi too, though those sons of my second wife do not show as much promise as these of my first.

As if in agreement with his thoughts, the voice of his second wife sounded through the partition, scolding her son on the other side of their duplex hut.

"Yapa! You stupid boy! You nearly pushed your little brother into the fire! Will you learn to sit still when you are inside?"

They are all my sons, thought the Bossboy, seed of the same man. I made them all. Two different women simply provided the sacs for them to grow in. Why aren't the second wife's sons as smart as the first wife's? He shook his head at this puzzle beyond his comprehension.

Meanwhile Toropo, too, stared into the fire and thought on her father's words, "Never forget a grievance." She wondered if he had any idea how great the hurt she nursed against him, because he would not let her go to school. She thought of the numerous times she had begged and pleaded to be allowed to go. But her father was adamant. "No! Boys need to learn the language and ways of the white man, and how to get money. But girls only need to learn how to plant gardens and care for children and pigs. You can learn from your own mother at home." Even Bani had often teased their father to let her go, telling him of the girls who were in school, and being careful to hide the fact that the ratio of girls to boys in his own class was one to eleven. However *Ara* had never yielded and now Toropo knew she was too old to go to school.

Suddenly both Toropo and her father's reveries were broken by a distant yodel.

"It's Turi!" breathed Toropo with relief.

"Turi! Turi" shouted Teni scuttling rapidly through the open doorway.

Out in the yard he gave a childish yodel, "Turi-yo-iyo-iyo!"

"Not bad," grinned his father at his mother. Her dark eyes shone a happy response to her husband's pride in their son.

"Turi-yo-iyo-iyo!"

"Even better," commented Pombo.

"Teni-yo-iyo-iyo," came faintly across the gorge. Turi had descended to the same height on the opposite side of the river as their house on this side.

"He heard me! He heard me! What do you know, he heard me!" shouted the happy little boy outside their door. His parents could hear the soft thud of his bare feet on the earth as he jumped with glee.

Toropo's torch had just caught flame. "Come on, let's go!" squealed Teni as she emerged from the hut.

The *pitpit* torch lit the way down the winding trail to the river below. Turi reached the river soon after they did and Toropo held the flaming cane to light his way across the long single-log bridge that spanned the rushing river. Together they climbed the steep hillside to their home, Teni chattering all the details about his possum until he was too breathless to say more.

"We were concerned about you, *nanga magol*," said his father as Turi grinned a shy greeting at them and sat down by the fire.

His mother handed him his favorite kind of *kaukau*. He smiled his appreciation. "I started late, *Ara*. I worked a couple hours after school in the banana orchard."

"You worked instead of coming straight home?"

"Yes, all the boys in our dorm did, along with our dorm parents."

"You know I commend your ambition, *magol*, but couldn't you work some other night when you'd be staying there anyway?"

"Yes, we have. We worked every afternoon this week."

"I see. What are you trying to earn?"

"There are special meetings next week including a big *mumu*. Mr. Jones is killing a cow and our dorm father is killing some chickens. The boys in our dorm voted to work this week and next to earn some meat."

"I see. It wouldn't matter if it weren't for Torombaiyo living beside the trail, you know."

"It was still daylight when I passed his place."

"I realize that now, of course, but I didn't know it yet when it got dark, you understand?"

"Well, he's home now," put in *Ama*.

"Yes, I just hope you won't do it again, Turi."

"I won't, *Ara*."

"Turi, how will Mr. Jones kill the cow?" asked Teni.

"He'll shoot it with a gun."

"Does he have a gun?"

"No, but he'll borrow one from the village magistrate. *Aya,*" continued Turi, turning to his only sister, "do you suppose you could come to Kauapena next week and bring me some more food for the *mumu*? If you could come on Wednesday I would like some fresh greens and *pitpit* to add to the feast."

"I'd like to," answered Toropo, delighted at the thought. It was always fun to visit the mission station. She had been so busy making gardens for the *singsing* that she hadn't been there yet this year.

"I guess you could," said her father. "Just make sure you leave plenty of everything for the *singsing*. We won't want to be short then."

"We won't be," assured *Ama*. "Toropo has a tremendous garden, and my own are good enough."

"Do you suppose I could have a stalk of cooking bananas, *Ara*?"

Ara deliberated with drawn brows and pursed lips. "I guess, maybe. There are two stalks that may ripen before the *singsing* anyway. You may have one of them."

"*Tsingo-we*! that will be great! I can pay back some of the gifts of food given to me. And I can make more gifts for boys to pay me back later!"

"Are you coming to *Ama's* garden with me tomorrow to catch that possum?"

"*Kapogla, ango*! How right we are to call you 'Bright Eyes.' This is the second possum you have tracked down in the month of July."

"July, July," chanted Teni. What a lovely foreign sounding word.

"You say it well," encouraged Turi. "Say some more. Try January."

"January," echoed Teni.

"February."

"Pebuary."

"No, February."

"F-February!" Toropo was trying the words with her little brother.

"Well, I'm off to the manhouse," declared *Ara*. "There will be a card game starting soon."

"Sleep well," grinned his wife, knowing he would probably play cards all night.

"Yes, all of you sleep," returned *Ara* as he crawled through the door.

"Look what I brought you, *Aya*," said Turi as soon as their father was gone. He slipped an exercise book out of his shoulder bag.

"Oh, Turi, how nice!"

"It's my Written Composition notebook. I filled it up this week so the teacher said I could bring it home." He opened to the first page. "See, I tried to write plainly so it would be easy for you to read."

"It looks so neat and nice. What's that word?"

"Children."

"What does it mean?"

"*Balkangoma* in *ImboUngu*. *Pikinini* in Pidgin."

"But I thought '*balkangoma*' was 'boys and girls' in English."

"Well, you can translate it that way, but children is a shorter way of saying boys and girls."

"I wonder why they don't say girl-boys like we do."

"English is different. They never say girl-boys to mean children."

"The children are playing," read Toropo. "One boy has a ball. What does 'has' mean?"

Teni tried repeating some of the sentences but soon grew bored and sleepy. The rain whispered a soft lullaby on the grass roof.

"I want to sleep, *Ama*."

His mother spread a leaf umbrella-mat on the floor near the wall. Teni curled up on it and she spread her *laplap* over him. He slept instantly. But the baby was wide awake and staring at his brother's red shirt. He reached out and grabbed a fistful of it.

"Look, *Ama*. He's reaching for me. He never did that before."

"He likes your shirt. Yes, he is noticing things and people more all the time now."

Turi took his baby brother on his lap. The baby immediately grasped the shirt in both little fists and tried to get it into his mouth.

"What is this word?"

"Toy. The boy has a toy truck," Turi read and translated. He fished around in his shoulder bag again and came up with a little hand mirror.

"Look what I have, *ango kogol*."

"Where did you get that?" asked *Ama*.

"I traded for it last Monday."

"What did you give in exchange?"

"Half of my week's *kaukau*." The boy ducked his head sheepishly. "Didn't you notice how hungry I was when I got here?"

"If you can get along on half the amount I won't need to send so much for next week," threatened *Ama*.

"Aw, *Ama*, you know I'm always hungry. But I wanted this mirror so badly I just had to trade."

"Why didn't this boy have any *kaukau* on Monday? I could understand if it had been the end of the week."

"His mother is dead. He never has enough to eat."

"How did an orphan boy get a mirror?"

"I asked him that. He said his older brother gave him the *kariyapa*, but he probably stole it. I kept it hidden all week just in case. I'll leave it here with you this week. Look, *Ama*. See how he likes it."

"*Kariyapa, kariyapa,*" cooed *Ama*. The baby looked at her and back again at the mirror. "*Kariyapa,*" said Turi. The baby looked at him.

"I know! Let's call him *Kariyapa*! That would be a good name. He needs a name, *Ama*. Look how big he's getting. The foreigners name their babies as soon as they're born."

"I know. Your brother told me that when Teni was a baby. I still don't think it's wise. Perhaps they don't fear the spirits like we do."

"No, God takes care of them."

"What? Don't their babies ever die?"

"None that I know of."

"Well, our baby is probably big enough. His fontanel doesn't pulsate so obviously any more. He's not as weak as he was at birth, certainly, but I waited longer than this to name you and Bani and Toropo. Teni was named earlier though, to please

Bani. The spirits didn't get him. *Kariyapa* would be a nice name."

So that was settled.

"*Kariyapa*," called Toropo. The baby turned to look at her. "He is definitely ready for a name. I almost think he knows it's his name already."

Toropo watched her two brothers.

"Turi, what does 'Some day you'll hear me calling' mean?"

Turi looked surprised, but translated it after a few seconds of thought. Now it was Toropo's turn to look surprised.

"And what about this: 'Promise me you'll answer. Promise me true'? I know the Pidgin words *'pramis'* and *'mi'* and *'tru'* but what is 'answer'? And what does it mean all joined together?"

Turi translated. Toropo thought her heart skipped a beat.

"Where did you hear those sentences?"

"There's a fellow named Peter staying with the catechist. He plays the guitar and he sings better than anyone I know. He sang that song to me. The tune keeps going over and over in my mind, but I can only remember that much.

"Some day you'll hear me calling," she sang. Then she hummed the second line. "Promise me you'll answer. Promise me true."

"Say, that's pretty."

"Will you come with me to hear him sing tomorrow afternoon, after you have helped Teni kill and eat his possum?"

"*Kapogla, Aya.*"

"I don't like it when Peter talks to me. He seems so bold or forward or something when he talks. But I can't resist his singing."

"I'll be glad to go with you. I'd like to hear him too."

"How long is he staying?" asked *Ama*.

"A few days, he says."

CHAPTER THREE

Wednesday morning the sun rose in crimson splendour. Toropo had been up for an hour already, and had eaten a good *kaukau* breakfast. Now she was ready to depart.

Her mother lifted the huge *bilum* of *kaukau* onto her head for her. Next she put the smaller *bilum* of *pitpit* shoots, spinach and cress on her daughter. Last of all she added the two-foot stalk of bananas.

"That's a fearful load to carry such a long way!"

"I'm young and strong, *Ama*."

"I still think you shouldn't take quite so much *kaukau*."

"I want a blouse so badly. I'm willing to work a bit hard to get it. Aren't you glad for me that it's not raining?"

"Yes, my daughter."

"Don't worry, *Ama*. I'll see you late this afternoon."

Toropo picked her way slowly down the steep hillside. At the river bank she stopped to check that her load was in perfect balance before she started across the single pole. Trudging up the other side, she stopped a couple times, half-leaning and half-sitting on a ledge to rest her head and neck. A smile flitted across her lips now and then, in spite of the intense physical labor. How she anticipated the new blouse, and here was something else too ...

The catechist had sent for her father Sunday afternoon. Peter had cared enough to put his thoughts into action.

"What are you asking for her bride price?"

"At least eight pigs."

"You wouldn't take money?"

"Oh yes, I'd accept some money too."

"But would you accept money instead of pigs?"

"All money?"

"Yes."

"No pigs?"

"That's right. That's what we had in mind."

"No pigs!" Bossboy Pombo had groaned. No, he couldn't consider it. He wanted pigs, big pigs. Pigs that could multiply themselves by at least five in a year's time. He needed to buy a wife for his eldest son. He had even been entertaining some hope of buying himself another wife with Toropo's bride price. There were other young men in his tribe who needed wives. As chief, much of the responsibility of raising their bridewealth rested on him. He had nephews ready to marry. They were his obligation as much as his own son. No, he must have pigs.

Money could buy trucks, but he had heard trucks seemed to have a bad habit of breaking down. People who knew how to fix them were as rare as grass growing on rocks. Pigs were a safer means of exchange.

Consequently the catechist had had to tell Peter the matter was closed unless he could buy pigs with his money.

Peter was considering it. The first proposition was to go home and get the money; beg it, raise it, borrow it. It might take a long time.

He had said goodbye to her on Monday. *"Mi go wokabaut gen nau*, but this time in my wanderings I'm going to try to raise money and then I'll wander back to you. Do you know anyone around here who would sell me some pigs?"

"No, I don't know of any."

"Don't take too long, young man," warned her father. "I can't let my daughter wait for you. She'll go to the first man who offers me enough!"

Toropo was not too concerned. Peter belonged to a different world. How strange it would be to speak Pidgin to your husband all your life! And anyway, he half belonged to Keri, his Laughing Eyes. But he had not inquired about Keri's bride price as far as she knew. It was her price he had wanted to know.

Toropo reached Kauapena before eight o'clock. Except for the two deep gorges near Tona it was downhill most of the way. She went straight to Turi's dormitory.

"What a huge load, *Aya*! I don't need that much *kaukau*!"

"No, you take out what you want and I'll try to sell the rest. I want to get some more money to buy myself a blouse."

Turi took a few *kaukau* and put them in his room with the *bilum* of greens and the stalk of bananas.

"Do you know anyone who might want to buy all this?"

"I'll ask my dorm mother. She might want it."
She did.

Toropo walked with Turi to his classroom. "The store will open any minute now."

"I'll watch you in your classroom a while first."

The bell rang and boys came running from every direction. There were some girls too. Toropo watched the class for half an hour before she decided she could delay her desire no longer. She sauntered slowly over to the tradestore.

Toropo considered the array of *meri* blouses. She immediately knew which one she wanted: one of those bright red ones with the big yellow flowers on it. She laid out her money. She had forty *toea* extra!

"How much is that yarn?" she inquired. "Twenty *toea* each."

"I'll take a red one and a white one."

Her purchases completed, she stood for a few minutes examining all the lovely ware and watching others buy. Then she meandered out and around the store building. Once she was hidden from view she quickly slipped her *bilum* and *laplap* off her head and put on her new blouse. She took up her *laplap* and wrapped it around her legs, tucking the top into her *purupuru* string. The red wraparound *laplap* gave a straight skirt effect and the full *meri* blouse gathered on a yoke accentuated it just right. Toropo both looked and felt attractive. She re-combed her hair, and strolled back to Turi's classroom with her *bilum* over one arm.

From her position near a window she became completely absorbed in the lessons. She repeated the Language Drills after the teacher in unison with the class, delighting in the sound of her own voice speaking English. In no time the class was dismissed for recess. Turi was beside her in a flash.

"Say! You look real nice, *Aya*. You look a lot like one of the teachers here."

"Who?"

"Nancy Wembi. She's the first grade teacher."

"Point her out to me if you get a chance, Turi."

Absorbed in their conversation they did not notice Turi's teacher approaching until he was beside them. Turi started but Toropo lifted her face calmly to look at him. Her eyes and smile were still radiant from her brother's compliments. The young man was struck with her beauty.

"Is this your sister?" he managed to ask Turi as he laid his hand on the little lad's shoulder.

"Yes, sir. This is my sister, Toropo."

"I noticed you listening to our lessons. Would you be interested in coming in to visit the classroom?"

"Oh, I'd love to if it wouldn't be a bother." Toropo's mind was in a turmoil. What was there about this young man's manner that was so unusual? So striking?

"Come in and I'll show you around the room." He went back to the door and motioned her to follow.

I know, she almost said aloud, as the thought struck her. He treats me as an equal. How strange for a man to speak to a woman in this way, and especially for an educated man to a bush woman.

Meanwhile, Turi had grasped her by the hand and was leading her into the classroom. Toropo rose to the occasion. If he treats me as an equal, then I must act like I am on his level and not giggle like a silly girl, she decided.

She listened to his explanations of charts, children's drawings and handcrafts attentively, commenting intelligently when given the opportunity.

"I like that drawing over there. The one entitled 'The children are playing.'"

"You read English?" asked the teacher, amazed.

"Only a very little," she smiled.

"Where did you learn?"

"From my brother here," she laid her arm around Turi's shoulders, "and from my older brother before him."

"Who is your older brother?"

"Bani. He's in Form Four at the Ialibu High School."

"Oh, I see. I've never met him. I'm new to the Southern Highlands. I just came this year. My name is Yurumbagi."

"Oh, is it? I thought it was Mr. Kasi. That's what Turi calls you."

"Ah, yes, that's my surname. My father's name, you understand. In Teacher's College they told us we must always have our students call us by our surnames."

"Oh, I see. And Yurumbagi is your real name."

"Yes." He loved to watch her face as she spoke. Her expressions fascinated him. "And your name is Toropo. Toropo Pombo."

"Mm," assented Toropo and turned away shyly to study a drawing.

"Mr. Kasi," ventured Turi timidly, "Toropo would like to see Mrs. Wembi. I've been telling her about her. Would you take her to her?"

"I'd be pleased to!" He led them to the doorway and invited her to precede them through it. She could not. A woman must always walk behind a man. Toropo could not bring herself to step in front of him and go out first.

Fortunately Turi saved the day. His teacher's word was law to the little fellow and he dare not let his sister disobey him. He pulled on her hand and led her through the doorway in front of Mr. Kasi.

Outside, without thinking, Toropo paused to let Yurumbagi pass her, intending from sheer force of habit to walk behind him. But when he asked her to walk beside him she complied. They crossed the assembly ground to the first grade classroom.

"Nancy," called Yurumbagi at the door. "Ah, yes, Yurumbagi," she answered, coming toward them.

"My student, Turi, wants his sister to meet you. Her name is Toropo."

"Why, how nice," she smiled, as the two women studied each other in a friendly way. "I was just putting a few sentences on the blackboard. Now I'm ready to go home to my baby. How about coming along for a cup of tea?"

"Ai, just the thing! Eh, Turi?" Yurumbagi accepted for all three.

Turi was thunderstruck! All because of his pretty sister he was being invited into the world of his teachers. Tea at a teacher's house! Wait till he told the boys!

Toropo managed superbly. None would have guessed that it was her first time to enter a Western style home with wooden walls and an iron roof. She watched Nancy carefully and followed her every cue.

"I could watch her for a year and never stop learning," thought the dazzled girl.

Nancy introduced Toropo to her husband, and allowed her to hold their baby, Nicky. Dressed in a snow-white nappie and little red shirt, Nicky delighted Toropo. He's exactly *Kariyapa's* age, thought Toropo. How cute *Kariyapa* would be, dressed in a nappie and shirt.

Nancy poured the tea. Yurumbagi took Toropo's cup, added sugar and handed it to her with a flourish. She accepted it gracefully with a slight smile at the raised eyebrows of Nancy and her husband.

"Thank you, sir."

The day passed all too swiftly and in no time Toropo was climbing the hills homeward. How delightful her taste of school life had been. She had enough memories to keep her mind busy pondering for weeks. Her feet fairly danced up and down the hills and she was home in two winks of the imagination. Finding no one there she continued on up the trail in the direction of her mother's garden. As she passed the turnoff to Tona Village she caught sight of a group of young people a short way up the path.

"Ai! Who's that?" called one of the boys.

She stopped and answered, "Who's yourself?"

"Why it's Toropo!" exclaimed Keri rushing down to her. "Your blouse is gorgeous, *Konopu!*"

"I'm happy with it," smiled her friend.

"You don't look like one of us," said one of the boys with a sneer.

Amazed at the tone in his voice Toropo turned and looked at him sharply.

"She thinks she's a white lady prancing up the trail," he continued in an aside to one of his friends.

"Come, Keri, let's go meet my mother and help her carry the *kaukau* or the baby. The rain is coming down river there." Toropo decided to ignore the boy. Nevertheless as she and Keri proceeded down the trail, a little of the joy in her blouse and happy day receded.

CHAPTER FOUR

The following day Toropo worked long and hard in her garden to make up for the day she had taken off. Pleasant memories flooded her mind as she dug. New dreams began to take form in her imagination. Often a soft smile parted her full red lips.

The precious blouse was hidden carefully at home, in the plastic bag in which the storekeeper had put the yarn. She did not want to get it dirty and sweaty right away.

What if it doesn't wash well, she worried. She had seen enough clothes to know that some never looked nice once washed, while on others the colors never ran or faded. I wonder if there is a way to tell what it is going to do, she pondered. If so, one could check before they bought anything. I must ask Bani when I see him again. He has worn clothes for ten years now. He probably knows.

It was nearly dusk when Toropo finally loaded the *kaukau* on her head and started homeward through the drizzling rain. It was hard to keep her bare feet from slipping on the wet trail. As she approached their hut in the darkness, she could see the firelight through the open door. Her mother and the boys were already inside. Then she heard her father's voice also.

She coughed as she lifted down her load to let them know she was there. In two minutes she had put both of her *bilum*s inside and was seating herself by the inviting fire.

"So this is the girl who wears clothes, is it?"

Toropo looked up in quick surprise at her father's unpleasant tone.

"You are the one who covers your body, are you?"

"Why, *Ara*, what's the matter with that?"

"Is there something wrong with your skin that you want to hide it?" Bossboy Pombo yelled.

"Who told you about my clothes, *Ara*, and what did they say?"

"The young men told me. They asked me the same thing I asked you. Is there something wrong with your skin that you have to hide it?"

Toropo dropped her head. Her father knew there was nothing wrong with her skin.

"Is there?" he yelled. "What's the matter with your skin? They promised me that they would spread the word around that Pombo's daughter has frog's skin from too much bathing and swimming like a boy, so now she has to cover it with clothes."

How he bristled!

"How many men do you suppose that sort of talk will bring round to discuss your bride price? Who do you think you are, to bring your father such shame?"

That stung.

"But *Ara*, I had no idea you'd mind. Remember the blouse you bought me once when I was a little girl? How was I supposed to know I couldn't buy myself one now?"

"Don't go making excuses. The past has nothing to do with the present."

Toropo was aware of people gathering outside. Why did her father have to yell so loudly? Yapa and Yombi, her two half-brothers, slipped in the door and sat down, followed by their sister, Mombo. She knew their mother and perhaps others were just beyond the doorway listening.

"But, *Ara*, I don't understand," she murmured, her head still lowered.

"What's the matter? Has your brain become water-logged as well as your body? Am I now trying to reason with a frog-brain?"

Silence.

"Don't you realize you have grown up since I bought you that other blouse long ago? Then you didn't have any breasts to cover up! I wasn't trying to hide you. There wasn't anything to hide. But now it's a different matter! Men are trying to see you. They want to know if you'd be worth buying. Why else do you think you have been nourished and cared for all your life?"

Toropo was thoroughly chastened. Her head sunk further down. "*Ama* wears a blouse when she has one," she mumbled.

"That's a different matter altogether! I might as well be trying to reason with a frog!"

A young passer-by came and sat in the doorway. Pombo never even paused to catch a breath.

"Your mother isn't on the market! I'm not trying to sell her. What do I care if she covers her body or not? I can see it when I want to. It makes no difference to me whether she hides it from other men or not. Men aren't interested in a woman's breasts after she has nursed six children. It's your fresh untouched breasts they want to see."

Could he humiliate her any further? Toropo had pulled her *laplap* around to hide her face and the tears that were running down her cheeks and dropping onto her breasts.

"Now I ask you again, where is this beautiful blouse?"

Toropo knew better than to tell him. He would rip it to shreds. She had worked too hard to earn it to sacrifice it to his anger.

Suddenly her father snatched the *laplap* from her head and hand and swatted her sharply across the face with it.

"Answer me!"

"Keri has it. I lent it to Keri. She wanted to wear it for a day."

"Well, just let her keep it then. I don't want to see it on you, do you hear? I don't want to even hear of it being on you!"

His anger subsided suddenly.

"I haven't seen it yet and I don't want to see it again," he added for the benefit of his audience. They laughed uproariously.

Toropo sat still. Tears continued to drop onto her legs but no sound of weeping could be heard. Teni and *Kariyapa* were huddled against their mother in fear. Their mother remained as silent as her daughter.

Bossboy Pombo turned and crawled through the door. The onlookers followed, joking loudly.

"Send my *kaukau* to the manhouse with Yombi, women," the Bossboy called back as he left the yard.

Yombi carried it to him that evening and both Friday morning and evening. He did not even come around as usual to await Turi's arrival.

Late that evening Toropo and Turi were sitting by the fire studying. Their mother and brothers had retired. At last Toropo laid the book aside.

"That's enough for tonight, I guess. You must be tired."

"*Aya*, I was waiting till the others were asleep to tell you that Mr. Kasi has been asking lots of questions about you yesterday and today. He wants you to come and visit us again next week."

"I'm going to be awfully busy until after the *singsing*, Turi. *Ara* will be upset with me if I go again before then. After that we'll see."

"*Kapogla nagol* … he will be disappointed, I know."

Toropo gave her brother a sad smile. "I'm sure he'll get over it. What sort of questions does he ask?"

"He asked if anyone has marked you for his own yet. He asked me if I knew how much *Ara* is asking for you. He wanted to know if you liked anyone and other things like that."

"What did you answer?"

"No to the first two. I told him I didn't know if you liked Peter or not. I told him about the songs Peter sang to you last Saturday."

"Hmm."

"*Aya*?"

"Yes?"

"You … you were so happy last weekend and then again Wednesday at Kauapena. Why are you so sad and quiet now?"

"Do I act sad?"

"Yes."

"I've tried not to."

"You've *tried* not to! Why do you have to try not to be sad? What's the matter?"

"Oh, there was a fuss over that *meri* blouse I bought."

"But why?"

"*Ara* has forbidden me to wear it."

"But why?"

Toropo shrugged.

"You looked so pretty in it, *Aya*. Did *Ara* see you in it?"

"No, and he doesn't want to again." She smiled a little through the tears gathering in her eyes.

"But I don't see why!"

"Neither did I so he called me a frog-brain."

"Aw, *Aya*!" Tears of sympathy gathered in the little boy's eyes as well.

I am thankful he doesn't have to know the worst of it, thought Toropo. Perhaps because of the mission school he will grow up thinking differently about girls. Maybe he will even learn to treat them like Mr. Kasi does.

"Mr. Kasi thinks you're real keen. He can't figure out how you learned so much without going to school. He says you beat the schoolgirls."

"Hmm."

"Want to hear what else he said?"

"Yes."

"He saw a play of the royal family when he was in college. He said you remind him of the princess."

"How could I remind him of a princess?"

"In the way you walk and the way you hold your head, he said." A sentence Turi couldn't quite understand, and certainly couldn't translate, was on his mind. "One would think she had been born in a palace instead of in a hut in the heart of the highlands!"

"Thank you for telling me all this, dear little Brother. It helps a lot."

"I like to see you happy, *Aya*. You ought to always be happy!"

+ + + +

The next three weeks flew by on wings. Bossboy Pombo worked daily with his men completing the longhouse which would house all the guests, gathering huge amounts of firewood and digging *mumu* pits. This particular longhouse was three hundred feet long and ten feet wide. It crouched low to the ground like all their houses, and curved up and over a hill on one end, resembling a huge grubworm when seen from a distance.

The women worked from dawn till dusk gardening, gathering the right kind of stones for a *mumu*, and catching the pigs that were to be killed for the feast. Most pigs, excepting a few special pets, ran wild in order that they might hunt their own food. Gardens were fenced in, instead of the pigs. The pigs had the run of the whole countryside and did not require much hand feeding.

This was the reason some of the biggest pigs learned to like their freedom too well and were dangerous to try to catch when necessary. Often when a woman had tracked down such a creature she had to go and enlist help to get the rope on him.

"Even then my old boar wouldn't co-operate," reported Pombo's eldest brother. "The more I pulled on him the angrier he got. He kept trying to attack me. Finally I worked out a solution. I made my old woman walk in front of him, keeping just out of his reach. He fought and lunged to get at her the whole way home. The old lady's hair was standing on end nearly as straight as the old pig's bristles! But if she got too far ahead the old boar would stop and refuse to go any farther. I'd have to make her come back and bait him again. Often he would nearly get her on that first lunge after a halt. That taught her not to get too far ahead of us, believe me! We finally made it home but the wife hasn't been any too friendly since. She pouts and refuses to feed the critter. She says he can starve to death as far as she is concerned. I have to get one of the other wives to take his *kaukau* to him."

The manhouse had been full of laughter during this recital. The men voted it the best joke of the present moon and repeated it time and again around every fire.

CHAPTER FIVE

The day of the *singsing*! Tona literally hummed. Everyone scurried here and there. Friendly laughter and merry shouts filled the air. Perspiration flowed freely. Pombo killed six pigs of his own, as well as several for older men. In all, the three Tona tribes killed nearly two hundred pigs that day.

Pombo felled several of his with a single blow. He and his men guests singed the pigs over open fires and cut them into quarters.

Toropo, her mother and Mombo's mother caught the blood in three-foot lengths of bamboo, into which they stuffed cress and bush spinach. Separating the edible from the inedible of the stomach and intestines took time but nothing was wasted. Teni and *Kariyapa* each received a cleansed pig bladder for a toy. They made perfect water balloons.

Fires snapped and crackled the full length of the longhouse and *singsing* ground. Smoke filled the air. Stones popped continually while being heated on the fires, resembling a kettle of popcorn, amplified a hundredfold. Mothers tried to keep children out of reach of the exploding stones. Many an eye has been blinded by the hot stone fragments. Later the iris and pupil turn blue. Accordingly all blue eyes are called "cooled eyes."

Adult guests and children old enough to wield a bamboo peeler all busily peeled *kaukau*, taro and green cooking bananas. By eleven o'clock the pork and vegetables had been placed between layers of hot stones in the *mumu* pits and covered with banana leaves.

"Come on, Toropo. Let's go home and get you ready," said her mother.

Toropo took *Kariyapa* in her arms and jounced him happily. "Isn't this the most exciting day of your life?" she asked the baby.

They collected several items and sat down in the front yard. Toropo combed her hair high in a beautifully shaped Afro.

"I'll put two stripes of red paint across your cheeks diagonally toward your temples and a spot on your forehead and nose. I think that will be enough. I don't want to hide your pretty features." *Ama* took care to make the stripes parallel.

"Now stand up and I'll pour this grease over you." She held the gourd of warmed pig grease on her daughter's shoulders and let it trickle down, back and front. She rubbed and massaged Toropo's back until every spot was covered, then each arm and around to the front. Cupping her hand she poured more grease into it and held her cupped hand to each breast.

Ama regarded her daughter's bosom proudly. It's evident, *ltemo*, that I did a good job of massaging her little chest when she was a baby. She smiled at the memory of how concerned she had been lest she fail in that important duty. When she left the isolation-hut with her two-month-old daughter, she had consulted her husband's mother in the absence of her own.

"Did you get any milk from them?" the old one had asked.

"Yes, a little from each side though it did not look much like milk."

"I imagine you did well, daughter, but it won't hurt for you and me to continue it every now and then."

Another proof that they had done well lay in the fact that none of Toropo's *poroman* or contemporaries had matured any earlier than she.

Ama finished greasing her daughter's stomach, hips and legs.

"My girl, you are striking!" she could not resist saying, as she stepped back to examine her for spots she may have missed. "You are perfectly and beautifully formed. The Good Spirit, *Kuro Kelkawe*, has truly blessed me in giving me such a lovely daughter and five good-looking sons."

"Four, *Ama*. You don't know if your dead son is good-looking or not."

"I know he was a pretty little boy before the spirits struck him so I am confident he is a handsome lad in the spirit world."

"*Ama!*" Toropo remonstrated. It was not wise to speak of the dead.

"There, there, never mind. There is not a spot on you that doesn't glisten, clear down to your shapely ankles. I'll tie this shell around your neck and then you go into the house and put on your new *purupuru*."

Toropo had dyed the outer thirds of the grass in her new skirt black, leaving the middle third it's original light green, both in front and back.

"Do we wait here for your father to bring your feathers or do we go look for him?"

"Let's wait a bit, *Ama*" Toropo suddenly felt shy and not anxious to rush things.

Keri appeared on the path. She glistened with grease also. Red and yellow paint decorated her face and three white cockatoo feathers sprouted from her hair.

"Ready, *Konopu*?" she called gaily.

"Almost. I'm only lacking my feathers."

The two girls chatted excitedly until Bossboy Pombo came in sight. His vermilion nose stood out in his black charcoaled face. A cassowary tail topped his neat bigwig, the plumes of which hung nearly halfway down his back. His shellband, the mark of his chiefhood, spanned his brow.

"My gorgeous father!"

"My two beautiful emerging butterflies! If you didn't belong to my own tribe I would want to marry you myself!"

While speaking, Pombo began unwrapping the string from a bark case.

"I saved the best for you, my daughter."

He drew out an exotic King of Saxony bird of paradise plume. It was twenty inches long and as fragile and fine as the most delicate lace. The girls gasped at its beauty.

Pombo experimented with different positions of the feather in his daughter's hair until he found the perfect accent for both the feather and her fine features.

"There my *Ambo Mopene*, let us be off."

The procession of four started up the hill with Pombo, of course, in the lead, and *Ama* last. Only *Ama* was undecorated. Woman's hour of glory was short indeed. Let the girls savour theirs to the fullest while it lasted. Marriage would end it. Thereafter any taste of splendour they enjoyed must be vicariously through their children.

They paused on the hilltop to look down on the *singsing* ground. It was a mammoth nest of exotic birds. Red, black, white, yellow and green plumage on several different shades of glistening brown. Three more descended.

Dancers stood in dance formation. Onlookers surrounded them. The drummers began to beat a rhythm on their long kundu drums.

The soloist led out in the chant:

"Now we are ready to dance!"

A hundred voices joined in on the yodel:
"*iyo-o iyo-o iyo-o*
"Notice our painted bodies,
"*eyo-o eyo-o eyo-o*
"Observe our glorious feathers!
"*eyo-o eyo-o eyo-o*
"We led a mighty hunt
"*iyo-o iyo-o iyo-o*
"To the big bush on our mountains.
"*iyo-o iyo-o iyo-o*"

The dancers were bobbing up and down in rhythm with the drums and yodelling chant.

"We trapped the mighty cassowary
"*eyo-o eyo-o eyo-o*
"The great bird that will claw you,
"*eyo-o eyo-o eyo-o*
"The bird that will disembowel you.
"*iyo-o iyo-o iyo-o*"
"We brought down the bird of paradise!
"*iyo-o iyo-o iyo-o*"
"The glorious males of paradise!
"*eyo-o eyo-o eyo-o*
"We felled them with our arrows,
"*eyo-o eyo-o eyo-o*
"Our swift straight four-pronged arrows.
"*iyo-o iyo-o iyo-o*"

The soloist could go on for hours, sometimes repeating age-old chants learned from his elders, often ad-libbing to fit the present occasion. When his voice gave out there was a stand-by ready to take over.

Sometimes the rhythm of the chant and dance was speeded up as the story reached a climax. The tempo of the drums kept pace.

Sometimes the dancers bobbed; sometimes they jumped. Sometimes they stood in lines, at times they formed a huge circle.

Ninety percent of the dancers were men. The other ten percent consisted of the young debutantes or butterflies who were making their formal eruption from the cocoon of childhood.

Toropo danced beside her father, studying the observers who were scrutinizing her. Many men stopped to stare long and hard at her. Sometimes the lust in their eyes made her drop her own in shame. At other times the open admiration of some made her eyes glow and encouraged her to greater effort in her dancing. Toropo knew many of the people but more were strangers.

Then Toropo happened to glance into the eyes of a man whose stare made her shudder. She dropped her eyes and analyzed her feelings. His eyes were full of lust, certainly, but many others were just as lustful. Why should her heart seem to stop at his gaze? Why should dread overwhelm her?

She danced on for ten minutes more before she ventured a look out of the corner of her eyes under drooping lids. She had lost all heart for dancing and the minutes seemed hours. She willed him to be gone but there he stood. Through half-closed lids with her head still turned to the right and her eyes to the left, she studied him. He was years older than her father but not quite as old as her grandfather. His gray beard bespoke his age. His "bigwig," not big at all, confirmed it because only old men wore such small wigs. Men who have had to admit that the bigwigs give them headaches, due to their size, weight and unwieldiness. He had not quite degenerated to the mere woven hat her grandfather wore, but the hair inside his wig was so inconsequential it was only a step away from it. Besides, it was lop-sided. It drooped behind his left ear. How revolting, thought Toropo.

She looked again at his eyes and again her heart choked with fear. His eyes, she realized now, said not only, "I want you," but also "I will have you!"

She turned and looked him fully in the face, her eyes wide open now, determined to cow his look, willing herself to defeat his self-confidence. They stared at each other for a full minute, her gaze shouting defiance, his speaking calmly of determination and self-assurance.

He out stared her. She had to look away first. As her eyes slid slowly away from his they fell on something else that jolted her. A girl stood there, only slightly older than herself. This girl was looking at her with black eyes so full of hatred that Toropo was astounded. No one had ever looked at her like that before. No one had ever hated her. Why should this strange girl hate her?

Toropo looked the girl over and slowly realized that she was pregnant though her stomach did not yet show it. She was merely fat. Toropo's mother had pointed out to her changes that took place in a woman's breasts during pregnancy. That meant that this girl was married.

Toropo turned away from them. She danced on, wondering about the girl and trying to forget the old man. Some time later her attention was diverted to a tall young man who was coming slowly but surely through the crowd of on-lookers straight toward her. A perfect bigwig, spanning two feet and topped with a cassowary headdress overshadowed his handsome face. He held his head high as though the weight of the wig and huge bird tail were nothing at all. Stopping in the third row from her where he could see her fully, his eyes on her were full of admiration, and even awe and reverence. They reminded her of Yurumbagi's eyes when he had handed her the cup of tea. But this fellow outdid Yurumbagi in looks and sheer male vitality. He's like *Ara*, she thought with surprise, only younger, taller, and more handsome ... or just as handsome anyway. She tried to be completely honest.

The young man stood there never moving, never taking his eyes from her. The crowd shifted and surged but he remained still, still and strong, sure as a rekari tree firmly rooted. She looked him fully in the face. She even allowed him little smiles though she well knew dancers were supposed to retain stoical expressions. She danced for him alone and she danced well.

Suddenly she recalled her other observer and glanced quickly in his direction. He was still there, as well as the girl who hated her. She tried to avoid direct contact with his eyes but she could not help noticing an amused expression on the old man's face. He raised his hand motioning her to stay, in the usual farewell expression, and smiled briefly. Then he turned and walked away. The girl who hated her gave her one final, belligerent look and followed him.

Ah, so she is his wife! Now I see. Why didn't I think of that? Old men often marry young girls. I just didn't connect them at first. Now I know why she hates me. She probably knows her husband pretty well and she must have seen the way he was looking at me. Once more a stab of fear pierced Toropo's heart.

Unconsciously she sought her young admirer's face for reassurance. He looked concerned. He must realize how scared I am, she thought. I am no good as a stoical dancer, *ltemo*. She gave him a faint smile to erase his concern and kept her eyes on him till the end of the dance.

What a relief when the dance finally ended! Now it was their guests' turn to demonstrate their ability.

Toropo turned wearily toward the long-house. Was it the dance or her own emotions that had tired her so? Anyway she was glad to be off display, sitting in the shade of the little brush arbor. She didn't care if she ever danced again!

"You danced well, daughter," *Ama* said as she passed Toropo her *bilum*.

Toropo immediately took out her water gourd. "Dancing in the *big-sun* makes me ready to die of thirst."

"And ready to rest, too, I imagine."

"Yes, I'll be ready to sleep tonight."

She had only rested a few minutes when her cousin, Koyaiye, came walking up with the tall young man who had watched her dance.

"Small Mama," said Koyaiye, addressing *Ama*, "This is Poropa. He wants to meet you and Toropo. He already talked to Small Papa. Small Papa told me to bring him to you."

"Fine. Fine. Sit down, young men."

They squatted on their haunches and Poropa turned to Toropo. "I saw you dancing. You were great!"

Toropo ducked her head. She didn't know what to say.

"*Inap long yumi tanim het long biknait?*" (May we have a date to turn heads tonight at midnight?) He looked first at

Toropo and then at *Ama*. "What does the Bossboy say?" asked *Ama*.

"He gave his permission."

"*Kapogla* then."

Poropa turned to Toropo. "How about it?"

She raised her eyebrows in silent assent.

"Good. We could gather at my Small Mama's house. That's Kewa-Ma. I'll come by and call for you late tonight. I know where you live."

After a pause Toropo said softly, "Kewa-Ma is from Kumunge."

"Yes, I'm from Kumunge. I've been away for three years though. I worked on a coffee plantation the other side of Minj. My contract was up on the first of July, so now I'm home. It's nice to be lazy and be my own boss again for a change. I sleep till noon and stay up half the night if I want to. I'm enjoying it."

Toropo wanted to keep him talking. "What's life like on a plantation?"

"It's work, work, work. But the pay is good. The housing and food are fine, but I got lonesome for my *wan-toks*. It seems mighty fine to be hearing and speaking my own language again."

"I don't think I would like to live where I couldn't hear anybody talk Real-People's-Talk (*ImboUngu*)!"

"No, I wouldn't want to for always either, but young men feel adventuresome, you know. It was nice to learn about more of the world, and to earn more money than I could have at home."

Toropo noticed the lopsided-wig man, watching her from a hundred feet away. The young girl still accompanied him.

"Are any of the rest of your family here?" she asked Poropa, thinking she must pretend not to notice Lop-Wig.

"Yes, my younger brother and sister and my father are here. We all decided to come when Kewa-Pa invited us to the *singsing*."

"Please point them out to me if they come in sight."

"That I will."

Toropo stole another sideways glance. Lop-Wig's back was turned to her as he spoke to his wife.

"Who is that old man, *Ama*?" she pointed in the usual manner, by squinting her nose in his direction.

"Him?" *Ama* likewise squinted.

"Yes."

"He's Kedle, from Piamble. Don't you remember him?"

"No, I don't. From when?"

"Oh, a few years ago when there was that big court case about Glopa-Pa killing his third wife."

"I remember the murder and the court sessions. But what did this Kedle have to do with it?"

"Do you remember the fellow that Glopa-Pa's third wife had committed adultery with?"

"Yes, I remember the fellow she was said to have slept with."

"Well, Kedle was called on to witness that the young fellow had bought a love potion from him."

"A love potion!" Toropo frowned in concentration. "And was he in trouble for selling him this love potion?"

"Oh, no. All he did was sell it. It wasn't his fault the man chose someone else's wife to give it to."

"And what happened to the young man? I can't remember."

"He was fined. He had to pay Glopa-Pa two pigs."

"And what happened to this Glopa-Pa for killing his wife?" asked Poropa.

"He was sent to jail for three years," Toropo answered. "He's been out since January. He was there dancing with us today."

"Show me which one he is sometime."

"*Kapogla*. Know what else he did before they put him in jail?"

"What?"

"He cut her body in pieces and sent a leg to one village, an arm to another, and so on, for all the young women and girls to see. He said we needed it for a warning of what will happen to us if we aren't faithful to our husbands."

"How awful! How old a woman was she?"

"Not very old. She had one child. My brother, Bani, would say she was still in her teens. Glopa-Pa says that since the white man's government has come to our land women are getting too much freedom. They must be shown that the old ways still hold—a man can still kill his wives if they look at another man. 'This newfangled business of jail! What's that matter?' he says. 'Who minds jail for three years if he can teach his wife a lesson?'"

"Did he talk any different when he got out of jail?"

"Not at all. He learned lots of things in jail. Now he likes to sleep in a bed so he made himself one. They taught him carpentry and he says he can earn more money than anybody else in our tribe now. He also says he ate fish and rice and lots of other foods three times a day in jail and that's better fare than three wives could feed him at home!"

"Well, I'll be!" Poropa fingered his well-kept beard. "I had a friend who was put in jail for three months. He really hated it. The worst thing I guess was having his hair and beard shaved off."

"Glopa-Pa says he didn't mind being shaved all that much. It was nice to be free of lice for a change, he said, like when he was a kid and would have his head shaved when they got too bad. Since there were none of his wantoks there to see him bald he wasn't too concerned."

"Perhaps a three-month jail sentence at the local government station is worse in some ways than a three-year sentence at one of the big provincial jails then," pondered Poropa.

The afternoon passed swiftly for Toropo and Poropa. Now the *mumu* was ready. Time to open the pits and take out the pork!

Bossboy Pombo, chief of the largest Tona tribe, was the first today to lift a large piece of roasted pork over his head and run yodelling down the *singsing* ground. As he handed over the pork to his debtor everyone had seen and could bear witness that he had repaid his debt to that man. Immediately another yodel began at the other end of the *mumu* pits and another man came running to another guest and debtor. These yodelling pork deliveries continued for nearly two hours.

Pombo had run out with so many gifts of meat that he was exhausted. He didn't make any more elaborate detours but ran straight to the receiver. When the pork was nearly gone Toropo's heart jumped into her throat at his next yodel:

"To Kedle, my friend Kedle-*yo-leyo-leyo*

Kedle of Piamble, father of Keledle - *yo-yo*
I bring this gift of pork *eye, eyo, eyo.*"

He walked rapidly to Kedle. Now why is he giving him a gift, she wondered. I'm sure he has never received pork from him. But he called him his friend. After the *singsing* I'll ask him about it.

They ate their pork and vegetables in the gathering dusk.

"The good Spirit, *Kuro Kelkawe* has given us a lovely day," said *Ama*, who was known to her friends as Bani-Ma. "Isn't it wonderful that we didn't have a drop of rain?"

The rain poured down with a vengeance when they were all in their homes that night. Lightning struck on a nearby mountain and the thunder rolled. Toropo, sitting by the fire with her *laplap* around her shoulders, suddenly snatched off her *laplap* and threw it against the wall. She had heard that lightning strikes people wearing red. It might be true and it might not, but she didn't want to be wearing it if the lightning were in a striking mood! Who wanted to be struck into the spirit-world on the night of her very first appointed head-turning?

She had watched many head-turning ceremonies during her childhood and recently she had even taken part in several, but only as a necessary extra.

A young man sat with a girl on either side of him. He leaned forward on the one side till his forehead touched the girl's. They swayed back and forth, foreheads rubbing. Then he turned to the girl on his other side and rubbed foreheads with her. The ultimate purpose was for him to choose one of the two girls for his own. Whenever Toropo had participated the fellows had all been local boys. She had not felt any emotion for any of them and it had all seemed rather silly. But now, the thought of turning heads with a man she knew she could love, a man she would like to marry, set her skin tingling.

Near midnight the storm abated. Out of the drizzle came the sound for which Toropo waited. The yodelling songs of young men. Soon Poropa was at her door.

"Come on, *Ambo Mopene*, lady fair, join us!"

Toropo slipped out with her umbrella-mat over her head and followed Poropa up the hill. They collected three more girls, still yodelling. It was wise to sing in the dark. One of Toropo's girlfriends had failed to call out often enough one night, and had been slashed by her own brother's machete. He had taken her to be a spirit. Toropo shivered in the darkness, but more from excitement than fear. Who could be afraid of spirits with Poropa near?

Once inside Kewa-Ma's house, Poropa, being the eldest as well as a natural leader, organized the group the way he desired. Girl, boy, girl, boy, and so on, beginning and ending with a girl. Not wanting to share his darling with anyone, he placed Toropo on one end with himself next to her.

Kewa-Ma built up the fire and played the part of chaperone. A crowd of children gathered from nearby houses to watch. *Ambo Kunana*, the love chant, began.

The first time Poropa placed his forehead against Toropo's and began the rubbing motion, a joy surged up in her chest so great it hurt, a delicious hurt. She forgot Kewa-Ma and the children and the words of the chant. She thought only of Poropa — the touch of his head, the smell of his body, the proximity of his eyes. If she opened her own she would be able to look straight into his, but she could not open hers. She enjoyed her emotions behind her shut lids, unaware that they still showed on her face in the firelight.

Then came the turn of the girl on Poropa's left. Toropo sat quietly, eyes downcast, while thrill after thrill of anticipation washed over her like waves.

During her third turn Poropa murmured softly, "Look at me, my love."

She intended to, but that delicious pain surged in her heart again so strongly she lacked the strength to move even her eyelids.

"Open your lovely eyes." The tone of command was strong in his subdued voice this time. Somehow she obeyed. The thick dark lids with the incredible lashes opened slowly. Poropa forgot to continue the rhythm and motion. His eyes were locked with hers. He was absorbed in their depths. They looked into his just a little fearfully, and yet at the same time trustingly. He felt as though he saw deep into her soul and the pure beauty of it made him catch his breath. He knew suddenly that she loved him. Such a love for her in return welled up in his own heart that he was amazed. He had not known he could love like this.

Poropa had turned heads with many girls. Passion and its satisfaction were no new thing to him. But the emotion he felt just now was entirely new. Such a tenderness for her overwhelmed him. He feared that it was unmanly and immediately resolved never to mention it to any man. At the same time he had a strong desire to watch over her and protect her from any harm.

Belatedly Poropa realized it must be time to switch girls. Glancing to his left he saw the girl watching him. "I got out of rhythm," he apologized.

When the *Ambo Kunana* had continued for two hours, onlookers began to depart for their own homes. The fire died down. Men chose the girl they preferred and couples paired off in the darkness of the hut for the finale of the date.

Poropa put his arm around Toropo and drew her closer to him. "Relax," he chuckled quietly. "I'm sorry the fire is out. I love to watch your eyes. I wish I could see them now."

Toropo's heart was thumping wildly. She hoped he could not hear it.

"But I know what they look like anyway," he murmured.

Toropo could not trust herself to speak. "Aren't you going to ask me what I think I'd see?"

"Mm," she managed to assent without opening her lips.

"I'd see fear."

He waited for her to deny it.

"I'd see love and trust but I'd see fear too. How can you fear me and trust me at the same time?"

Silence.

"I want an answer, little love." He cupped his free hand under her chin and turned her face to his in the darkness.

"I can't answer your question." Her voice was throaty.

"Try, my love."

He rubbed his cheek against hers and brushed her lips with his own. She caught her breath but did not pull away.

"I'm waiting."

"I trust you more than I'd trust any man," she answered in a rush, her breathing showing the effort it took her, "but I don't know men." She dropped her head and it rested on his shoulder. She was ashamed of her confession. She felt that he knew women.

Poropa smiled into the dark. He well knew this was her first experience with a man and with love. The wonder of it had been written all over her face.

"I know, my love, but don't be ashamed of it. It makes you all the more desirable to me."

He kissed her softly on the forehead, then chuckled quietly. "You trust me more than you would trust other men but you just don't know how far you can trust any man. Is that it?"

"Mm."

"Darling, you don't need to fear me. I wouldn't hurt you. I couldn't!"

Toropo sat within his embrace feeling loved and secure. What a wonderful man he was! *Kuro Kelkawe*, please bring about our marriage, she prayed. She was amazed at her own feelings, at the response of her body to his. Until tonight she would not have believed such a thing possible. And he would be tender. She knew he would. She did trust him completely.

As if he read her thoughts he said, "Let's meet together behind the bamboo at the far end of the *singsing* grounds tomorrow afternoon."

"No, Poropa."

He had known she would refuse. Neither would he force her just yet.

"But darling, your father and I have already arranged to discuss your bride price tomorrow."

"I'm glad, Poropa."

"It's as good as settled. I want you for my wife."

"I'm so glad."

"Will you meet me alone tomorrow then?"

"No, Poropa, please. Not yet."

"Let me sing to you again tomorrow night and maybe after that?"

"Maybe."

"If your father and I can come to an agreement? Promise me."

"*Kapogla*, Poropa, if you two can agree. I hope and pray he will accept what you offer."

"I, too. But if he doesn't, I'll find more somehow. I'd go back to the plantation to earn more but I know you'd be gone before I got back. I realize it's now or never."

All Toropo's fear vanished when Poropa accepted her refusal. She relaxed in his arms and accepted his caresses happily. She felt the most secure, contented and loved that she ever remembered feeling in all her life.

The bud had opened and experienced such joy in the opening that it had no desire to rush the flowering. The butterfly had emerged from the chrysalis. The air was so sweet on her wings! The freedom so wonderful! Why fly just yet?

She wondered if the other girls around her in the darkness were as reticent as she or were they arranging secret rendez-vous for the morrow? Never-mind, she was content and Poropa seemed content to wait.

CHAPTER SIX

Toropo awoke to the sound of breakfast. She sat up suddenly.

"There's the girl who danced for two hours and said she would be ready to sleep last night. And did she sleep? No indeed! She was up the whole night!"

"Oh, *Ama*!"

"The whole night, I tell you. She just caught two winks at dawn!"

"Aw, *Ama*, it was more than two winks."

"Two winks, I tell you. You came in at the hour-of-sweet-sleep just before dawn. I was awake."

"Truly? I feel rested now."

"Never mind, daughter. You're only young once. You only emerge from your chrysalis once in a lifetime. Did you enjoy yourself last night?"

"Oh, *Ama*, did I ever! *Paa-tsingo-we*! Poropa is just wonderful! I didn't know a man could be so nice, so great, so understanding, so sweet!"

"Truly?" *Ama* was grinning at all those adjectives.

"Truly, *Ama*. And guess what? He's going to talk to *Ara* about my brideprice today. You never know, *Ama*, by this time next month I might be married!"

"Hm. Maybe I ought to show him your garden."

Toropo laughed lightheartedly. "I don't think it's necessary."

"The young lady is quite sure of herself," *Ama* said to Turi.

"Poor Mr. Kasi. I'll hate to have to tell him."

"Don't tell him unless he asks," advised Toropo.

"You can be sure he'll ask."

The family ate all they could hold of food left over from the *mumu*. Guests and relatives came by and the day passed swiftly in happy conversation. On the *singsing* ground dancing continued. Toropo went with her maternal cousin to see the dancing at one stage, hoping she would see Poropa. After determining that he was nowhere on the grounds she returned to her home to wait for him to appear.

Late that afternoon she glanced up the trail to see Poropa slowly descending. She studied him concernedly. He seemed different from the day and night before. Perhaps he is tired, she thought.

He approached the corner of her yard where she sat with her cousin and half-sister. Without a word he sat down near her.

Toropo waited. As he still said nothing, she asked softly, "Are you tired?"

Poropa did not appear to have heard for some time. Finally he mumbled, "Tired. More tired than I have ever been before. Tired enough to lie down and die."

Toropo was deeply concerned. Her heart seemed to suddenly constrict in fear.

"Why, Poropa, why?"

"I cannot have you, my little love. You have already been sold."

Fear seemed to squeeze the breath out of Toropo. How could her heart go on beating with this band tightening around it?

"How? When? To whom?" She managed to force the words out through lips that seemed paralyzed.

"Just since I talked to your father yesterday. That man, Kedle from Piamble. I hate his guts!"

A cry of pure anguish escaped from Toropo's lips, "Kedle from Piamble!"

"Yes! The beast says he will have you for his tenth wife!"

"Tenth wife? *Tenth*?" Oh, *Kuro Kelkawe*, have mercy! Toropo thought she was going to pass out. She could not get her breath. That band seemed to squeeze her heart and lungs tighter and tighter. A low moan escaped from her as she leaned forward and rested her head on her knees. She remained in that position without speech or even thought, for some time. Then slowly as the blood returned to her brain, thoughts started flooding in again. Suddenly she sat upright.

"But is it final, Poropa? Can't you offer a higher bride price? He hasn't given *Ara* the pigs yet. Oh Poropa, help me! You've got to help me!" Her voice rose to a scream on the last sentence.

She was totally unaware of the friends and relatives who had gathered around.

"It is final, darling. There is no hope. There is nothing I can do. I tried and tried. Believe me, I tried. I argued and fought for you. But the Beast has offered fifteen pigs, five cassowary tails, fifteen shells and five hundred *kina*. Who can top that? And if anyone does he promises to raise his offer. He has promised five pigs more than any other man offers your father. If I could get fifteen pigs together, and darling I can't! That's enough for two wives you know. But if I could, your father wouldn't accept them, knowing he could get twenty from Kedle then, for you."

"By all the spirits of the dead, where can he get so many pigs?"

"Remember, he has nine wives growing gardens and raising pigs for him. Also, mind you, those wives are producing daughters. Your father says Kedle has already sold five daughters in marriage over the past few years."

"Five daughters already married?"

"What's more, he is the only man around who has the materials and recipe for the love potion. It was passed on to him alone by his father. His potions have the reputation of being the strongest, most potent, most effective of any man's in the Imbo-Ungu area. They are said to be effectual nine times out of ten. Who else can boast such a high kill? Men all over, and women too for that matter, will pay a high price for a potion so sure as that!"

Toropo groaned aloud.

"He is the *source* of pigs and *kinas*! Who else can compete? I'm going home, Love. I can't bear to stay around any longer. I only came to say 'Good-by.'"

"But it's too late to walk all the way to Kumunge now, Poropa. You better wait till morning, at least."

"I can't. I must be going. I can't bear to be near you, knowing you'll never be mine. I won't mind walking over strange trails in the dark. I'd welcome the spirits or enemy! Who wants to live without you anyway?" His voice broke and rising to his feet, he hurried from the yard, down the trail.

Toropo sat for a time looking after him, too stunned to move. At last she too rose to her feet and stumbled slowly around to the back of her hut out of sight of sympathetic onlookers. Slowly, without conscious thought, her feet sought out an overgrown path that led to a childhood refuge, a secluded spot under a clump of bamboo nearly five hundred feet below her home. She parted the overhanging willowy ends and sank down on the cool earth. For hours she lay there, too shaken even for tears. Finally she fell into an exhausted sleep.

At midnight she awakened. Realization came flooding in once again. She was chilled to the bone physically and chilled to the very heart emotionally. Drops of water had begun to fall from the soaked bamboo onto her bare skin. It must have been raining quite a while, she thought. Her *bilum* had fallen from her head unheeded, earlier. Now, groping in the darkness, she found it and withdrew her umbrella. Parting the bamboo with the upper point of her umbrella-mat, she made her weary way upward in the darkness.

The door was unlocked and her mother was sitting by a bright fire as Toropo had known she would be.

"My daughter," she whispered, as Toropo slipped in. She sat down a couple feet from her mother, putting both feet into the warm ashes and holding her hands to the blaze. After a few minutes of silence Toropo raised anguished eyes to her mother's face. Her mother's eyes were dark pools of love and sympathy. She's suffering with me, Toropo realized at once.

"Oh, *Ama!*" At last the tears welled up and overflowed.

Her mother slid sideways and took her into her arms, though the two had not embraced for years. She pressed her daughter's head against her bare breasts. Tears poured from Toropo's eyes in torrents as sobs racked her whole body.

Her mother's tears dropped on to Toropo's hair where they glistened in the black ringlets.

"My daughter, oh my daughter -iyo -iyo -iyo," cried her mother softly in a singsong chant, nearly like the death wail. "My daughter with all her beauty -yo. My daughter in her first love -iyo -iyo -iyo." *Ama* rocked back and forth, cradling her daughter's head with one arm and caressing her hair and back with the other hand. When the sobs did not abate, *Ama* began to sing a story.

"There was once a beautiful garden yo-iyo
A beautiful maiden lived within this garden-iyo
Lived among the beautiful trees and flowers-yo

Beautiful trees, flowers and bamboo-yo
-iyo-iyo-iyo-iyo-iyo"

Toropo's sobs lessened and she cried more quietly as she lay listening to her mother's chant.

"Once a handsome young man-iyo
Handsome young man happened by-iyo
Happened by the beautiful garden-iyo
Saw the maiden in the beautiful garden-iyo
-iyo-iyo-iyo-iyo-iyo

"He yodelled to the beautiful maiden-iyo
Yodelled and called to his fair lady-yo
Called and asked admittance to her garden-iyo
Asked admittance to her lovely garden-iyo
-iyo-iyo-iyo-iyo-iyo

"The maiden willingly admitted him-iyo
Admitted him to her lovely garden-iyo
To her trees, bamboo and flowers-iyo
To the very heart of her-*iyo-iyo*
-iyo-iyo-iyo-iyo-iyo

"He held her in his arms and loved her so
He looked into her eyes and worshipped-yo
Deep into her eyes where fires glow
Fires of love and passion-*yo-iyo*
-iyo-iyo-iyo-iyo-iyo

"Before their love was consumated-yo
Before she had drunk his love-*iyo-iyo*
Before he took her into his own soul
A snake came into the garden-*iyo-iyo*
-iyo-iyo-iyo-iyo-iyo

"Wormed his way between them-*yo-iyo*
Coiled himself around the lady fair
Poisoned her with his deadly fangs-*iyo*
Stunned her, dragged her off into his lair
-iyo-iyo-iyo-iyo-iyo"

An occasional tear still slipped from underneath Toropo's closed lids as her mother related the story of her defeated love in one allegory after another. At last, utterly exhausted, she was lulled to sleep by her mother's singing and rocking.

When *Ama* felt Toropo was sound asleep she gradually ceased her chant and motion and eased her head into a more comfortable position on her lap. She looked long and lovingly at her daughter's tear-stained face.

"My poor daughter, my only daughter, my baby girl. It's so hard, so very hard for you," she murmured. "I was fortunate to be bought by your father when I was your age. He was a young man, strong and handsome, virile. My heartbreak came later, when he took his second wife. I felt at the time that my heart had died, but I had it easier than you do. I was still close to the man I had learned to love. I only had to share him. The spirits know, that was hard enough!"

Fresh tears fell onto Toropo's hair.

"But you, my daughter, must never again see the man you could love. Instead you must go to a man who is older than your father, and share him with nine other wives! Nine others! Many are the girls who must go to older men but most of them are only third or fourth wives. Not that that may make it any easier. I don't know. It just seems to me that this Kedle has had more than his rightful share. Why should he have my pretty baby as well as all of his other nine wives?"

Ama gave her whole mind to praying to the Good Spirit, *Kuro Kelkawe* to avert the disaster. She felt no confidence that he would answer though unless he were offered a blood sacrifice. And she could not do that. Only men were worthy of offering sacrifices to the spirits. What was the good of even praying? One ought to do something however. It was no good standing by and watching your daughter break her heart without doing anything! But what could a woman do?

She finally fell asleep, sitting, leaning against the bark wall.

CHAPTER SEVEN

Bossboy Pombo did not visit his first wife's home the following day. He wanted to be certain that Toropo had time to learn of her marriage from someone else. However, the next morning he knew he must not put if off any longer. There were arrangements to make, things to be done before the exchange. He appeared at their door while *Ama* and Toropo were eating breakfast.

One glance at his daughter told him what he wanted to know. She knew. Someone had told her. She drooped like a poinsettia broken from its root. His heart smote him at this drastic change. He wondered if she would ever carry her head high again. But immediately Reason began telling Heart the necessity of this marriage. There was no other way. No turning back.

He seated himself at the fire and accepted a *kaukau* from his wife. Toropo began to nibble on the *kaukau* she held, to hide her discomposure.

"Kedle will be bringing the bride price Saturday," Pombo informed them.

Toropo gasped.

"Saturday!" exclaimed *Ama*. "So soon?"

"Yes, this Saturday."

"But this is Tuesday! We only heard of it Sunday!"

"I know, I know."

"There's no need to get in such a rush. It's indecent!"

"Not at all, woman. There's nothing indecent about it. Kedle simply has the pigs and articles all ready and he says there is no need to delay."

"He's afraid you'll change your mind. I've never heard of the price being agreed upon and exchanged in such a short time."

"He's not one of your poor men who has to go around canvassing the whole tribe, trying to scrape up a bride price. He has all he needs within his own family."

"His family would just about make a whole village."

"Right. So he's coming Saturday. So we must be ready," Pombo took a deep breath.

"I've promised him our sow, Pingi, for the exchange."

"Pingi! Pingi? Why Pingi? There's no need to give him my best sow! I'm sure he has enough of his own. Pingi is the only sow we've ever had that raised twelve piglets from one litter. Why did you promise him her, Man?"

"Listen, old woman! That sow will belong to your daughter. She will set up housekeeping with it. Would you begrudge her the best?"

"Ha! Belong to my daughter! Grubworms! Nothing ever belongs to any woman!"

"Of course it does. You own your own pigs."

"If I own them why did *you* go promising Pingi to Kedle without consulting me? You know I raised Pingi as a special pet. When her mother died I chewed sugar cane and *kaukau* and spat it into her mouth. When I saw she was going to die anyway, *ltemo*, I nursed her at my own breast. And yet does she belong to me? You up and promise her to that beast of a man without even telling me first."

"Kedle's no beast. He's a fine man. I admire him greatly."

"Ha! You admire his wealth! He's a beast and worse than a beast. He is as bad as any evil spirit in the spirit world. Pingi's too good for him! And yet you promise him our beautiful daughter. Fair as a flower she is, and pure as one too. All for that beast of a man who has known so many women that one more won't mean anything to him at all!"

"Now, now, calm down, woman. Settle down and let's talk sense. What do you have against Kedle?"

"His age, of course!"

"What about his age?"

"He's older than you are. He's old enough to be your father!"

"He's not as old as my father."

"I didn't say he was. I said he's old enough to be your father. You are your father's youngest child, remember. Your father already had a grandchild when you were born."

"All right! All right! Don't talk to me as though I were a child! Think of his wealth. His wealth easily outweighs his age.

It couldn't be an unpleasant thing to be married to such a wealthy man."

"What's wealth to a young girl? Our daughter loves a handsome young man and here she must go to this poor excuse for a man instead. He not only doesn't wear a bigwig but he can't even keep his little wig setting upright on his head!"

Pombo grinned. "Maybe Toropo can straighten it up for him." Then he turned to his daughter. "Is it true that you love a young man?"

Toropo made no response as she stared at the dying fire.

"*Paaimbo ltemo*," her mother answered for her. "She lost her heart instantly to that young Poropa from Kumunge."

"Give me one of those '*eat-it-raw's*,' Teni. I'm sorry to hear that, Toropo. But I can't let it change things. I can't go back on my word. If I weren't the Bossboy I might consider accepting less than the most I can get for you. But even then it's doubtful. A father shares the bridewealth with every male relation, with any man who has ever given his daughter so much as a bite of *kaukau*. You know that. As chief, it is my obligation to increase the wealth of my tribe as much as possible. Why, I'd be cross with my brothers if they accepted less than the most they could get for their daughters. Your brother, two of your cousins, and three other men in your tribe need wives. We have to have all we can get to buy them. I couldn't hold up my head if I accepted Poropa's price for you instead of Kedle's."

His wife eyed him scornfully. "And a man's pride is more important than a woman's heart and soul."

"Oh, go on. There's no reasoning with a woman!" He turned and crawled out the door. His wife was right on his tail feathers, or tii leaves.

"You call me an old woman. Perhaps I am. Perhaps I can die soon and come back and eat you. I took it without a word when you broke my own heart but I'd give my very life to keep you from breaking our daughter's."

Pombo climbed the hill unheedingly, it seemed, but he had heard every word. It's true, he thought, she never said a word to me when I took my second wife. She wilted and drooped much like Toropo has done. But she's going to fight like an old sow when one of her piglets squeals. Well, he shrugged, nothing can be done about it now. I wonder how she and the second wife will react when I take a third. I've wanted to for years. This extra big bride price for Toropo will make it possible. He walked on deep in thought. In the end he concluded he had better wait until there was a little more domestic peace.

"It's no use, *Ama*, we'll just have to accept it," said Toropo as *Ama* put Teni's noon *kaukau* into her *bilum*.

"I can't see your heart break and not try to fight for you, daughter."

"Tell me about the time you went through heartbreak yourself, *Ama*."

"Come to the garden with me, *nanga bagol kogol*, and I'll tell you while I dig *kaukau* for the pigs."

"*Kapogla*. I'd like that. I don't feel like going to my own garden today."

"No, there's no need. You only have four days here. Let's spend them together."

"Thank you, *Ama*, that will help a lot." Toropo sat playing with *Kariyapa* as her mother busily dug *kaukau*.

"Tell me, *Ama*."

"Well, it was like this. I hadn't known your father at all before we were married but I soon fell in love with him afterwards. We were only married a short while before I became pregnant for Bani. Your father was well-pleased that I gave him a son first. Those were the best years of my life. But before Bani was old enough to be weaned your father was urging me to let him sleep with me again. I refused until Bani was nearly Teni's age, as my mother had always advised me.

"Well, wouldn't you know, I got pregnant right off, again. It seems I breed as easily as Pingi and I never saw any sow to beat her for easy breeding.

"Then you were born, *nanga bagol kogol*, and your father wasn't pleased about you being a girl. He said a man wants two sons first in case something should happen to one.

"I had only been back from the isolation-hut a month when your father declared he was getting himself another wife. In desperation I told him we could sleep together.

"He was amazed and said, 'What about the baby?'

"It's only a girl,' I answered. 'You don't care if she dies.'

"He agreed and we began to sleep together regularly. I was pregnant again before you were four months old. Some say you can't get pregnant if you are nursing and haven't had your moon-sick, but don't you believe it. I did.

"Your grandmother and other women urged me to let them abort it but I refused. I had seen too many women die that way.

"So your little brother was born when you only had four teeth and were just toddling. I nursed both of you. People scolded me for it but I kept it up. I always let the baby nurse first, then when he had had all he wanted I let you finish it. You sucked and sucked until you had drained every drop. *Kuro Kelkawe* was good to me and increased my milk. You didn't get thin and your baby brother grew fat and flourished. I gave you lots of sugar cane to eat and I cooked your *kaukau* just as soft as I could get it. I loved you, *nanga bagol kogol*, even though your father had half turned from me ever since your birth. I did pray to the spirits though to never let me bear another girl child. I made the prayer at the same time the men were offering blood to the spirits with another request. Mine has been answered.

"As soon as your brother was born I had to refuse to sleep with your father again. Two babies were all I could manage at once. So he immediately went off in search of a second wife. Your baby brother was beginning to toddle before he exchanged the pay for Mombo-Ma though.

"I had worked so hard to please your father so he wouldn't get a second wife but I hadn't succeeded. My heart broke but somehow in the following years I worked harder than ever to show him I was the better wife. It wasn't hard to do really. Mombo-Ma has always been lazy. But because I was so concerned about my relationship with your father all those first few years of your life I'm afraid you didn't have a very happy babyhood. In after years I realized how I had neglected you.

"Until your brother got too big, I carried you both back and forth to the gardens along with my loads of *kaukau*. But soon he was as big as you were and I had to let you walk. You were better at walking than he, of course. You began to follow Bani all around and he was surprisingly good to you. That's why you two have always been so close. You grew up so fast. You could run and play and swim and do everything the boys did, even when you were so tiny."

"And then my little brother died when he was about Teni's age," put in Toropo. She knew that story.

"Yes, the spirits ate him and he died. I told your father the spirits were punishing him for not thinking of his son, for thinking about getting another wife instead. But in my heart I knew otherwise. They were punishing me for sleeping with my husband too soon after your birth, so they took away the object of that conception. It was fair. I should not have done it. I lost the battle anyway. Women can never stand against men."

"How did you feel toward Mombo-Ma, *Ama*?"

"I hated her, of course. She took my husband away from me."

"And just think, *Ama*. There will be nine women to hate me!"

The woman dug in silent thought. Yes, hating the next wife solved nothing. But whom should one hate then? It was impossible to take it without hatred and anger toward someone, something. No use hating your husband when you had to go on living with him and working to provide for him.

"Did you ever beat her or harm her in any way physically, *Ama*?"

"No, I never laid a hand on her. I feared your father too much to do that. I did say some pretty cutting things to her on occasion though and once your father came upon us unexpectedly and found her in tears."

"What happened then?"

"After he learned what I had said he warned me never to talk to her like that again or he would chop me in two with his axe."

"Did you ever talk like that again?"

"No, I didn't. I obeyed him."

"You think he really would have?"

"He surely would have. Don't you ever doubt it! He is just as capable of it as GlopaPa is."

"Do you suppose Kedle would be capable of it?"

"I don't know, daughter. You'll have to learn that for yourself."

+ + +

In the long, dark hours of night Toropo tossed and turned.

A loving voice murmured, "I'm wide awake, too, *nanga bagol kogol*, I'll be glad to listen if you want to talk."

Dread filled each hour, and yet the days passed all too quickly. Friday evening a messenger arrived from Piamble.

"Kedle sends word that he won't be able to come tomorrow. His ninth wife is very ill. He will come next Wednesday if she is better."

They talked around the fire. The fellow was friendly and willing to visit while he ate their food.

"What's the matter with the ninth wife?" asked *Ama*.

"Her ailment wasn't included in the message."

"But you know?"

"Yes, I know."

They chewed in silence before he finally spoke again with some hesitation. "Somebody performed an abortion on her. She nearly died yesterday. Kedle had to take her to the mission clinic as a last resort. She's still alive today, or was when I left at least, but the *ambo kondodle* says she is still critical."

Toropo thanked *Kuro Kelkawe* for the delay, but again the days flew by on wings. Perhaps the ninth wife will die and he will postpone our marriage while he mourns for her, she thought. But again that would only be a temporary reprieve. How much better it would be if Kedle himself would die! Accordingly she prayed to the evil spirits to strike him.

The evil spirits did not answer however. Kedle appeared at the Tona manhouse well and strong on Wednesday morning. A whole retinue of his tribe trailed behind him, leading the fifteen pigs. Toropo stole just one look at her husband-to-be to see if his hat and wig were on straight. No such luck!

The exchange proceeded without a ripple. Toropo's tribe was so pleased with the large bride price that there was none of the customary bickering. In no time Kedle and Toropo were standing before the chief of the second Tona tribe, with their little fingers crooked together, while he pronounced them man and wife.

Kedle gave the sow, Pingi, into the care of a woman unknown to Toropo and then motioned for Toropo to walk directly behind him. The others could fall in as they wished.

Toropo knew every detail of her husband's feet and footprints before they completed the two-hour trip to her new home. There were no deep gorges between Tona and Piamble but she became aware that they were climbing, gradually but steadily.

She fingered the lovely *bilum* she was wearing on her head, the marriage *bilum*. Her mother had worn it when she was married and her mother's mother before her. Her great-grandmother had made it and dyed it coal black. Whenever *Ama* had unwrapped it and shown it to her during her childhood, she had woven happy dreams around it. What had ever given her the idea that marriage was a happy occasion? She now knew it to be the most tragic occurrence of her life.

A *singsing* oval came into view and Kedle turned to her. "This is *Peyamo-peli*, the home of the Spirit Peyamo. Piamble takes its name from that spirit. Peyamo lives in that tree right there," he said, squinting his nose and pointing his chin at a huge tree.

They walked a little farther and came to a larger *singsing* area bordered on the upper end by a government road. Toropo wanted to ask if trucks and cars actually drove on the road, but she decided silence was the better policy for the present. She had long, dreary years ahead to satisfy her curiosity on all such matters. She lifted her eyes to the mountain which towered above them. Piamble nestled at the foot of Mt. Giluwe, the second highest mountain in Papua New Guinea.

Kedle pointed out a house on their right. "This is the home of the government medical orderly. We call him 'Dokta.'" Squinting to their left he continued. "And that is the Bible Mission station, just across this little stream. They have a nice store, a couple of school buildings and a clinic as well as all the houses in which people live. That longest building is the church. The big square one is the *kondodle's* home."

Toropo studied the tall buildings favored by expatriates with interest.

"I'll bring you down here to the store tomorrow to buy you some new clothes and things," continued Kedle.

Toropo was so surprised she glanced up at her husband. So she was to be allowed to wear clothes. Her precious blouse was hidden under other things in her marriage *bilum*.

Kedle turned and walked on. People came out of nearby huts to stare at Toropo and the bridal procession. He did not speak to her in front of them. They reached the government road, turned right and walked along it for one kilometer. Then they branched off on a trail to their left. In a few minutes they were standing on a hilltop looking at a large village of huts spread out on a hillside across a little stream from them.

"This is our home," said Kedle.

He waited while Toropo stood studying the outlay thoughtfully. She picked out the manhouse immediately right at the top of the village about three-fourths of the way up the hill. Each of the other huts must belong to the different wives and the smaller ones might be pig houses, she supposed.

He led her to a comparatively new hut, neatly made, small and compact, situated not too far from the manhouse.

"Someone will bring you food," he said, and left her there.

CHAPTER EIGHT

Toropo awakened before dawn as usual. She would have liked to have gone out and found a good vantage point from which to watch the sunrise as she often did at Tona, but she might meet someone. She built her fire and sat down to peel some *kaukau* like the matronly woman she was now supposed to be.

She was glad Kedle had left her in the night. He had been so thoroughly revolting that it was well she did not have to face him in the light. Her disgust would show in both her manner and expression, try as she might to hide it.

Toropo liked her neat cozy little hut. She looked around her with a sad pleasure. It was so new that there wasn't much soot on the inside of the *kunai*-grass roof yet. Soot. Pingi. That reminded her. Where was Pingi? I'm so lonesome that even the sight of *Ama's* pig would be a comfort.

Her *kaukau* was cooked and she nibbled at it slowly, lacking appetite. How I wish someone would come and talk to me. I'm going to go crazy sitting here alone.

Three hours later she was still thinking the same. At least I don't want Kedle to come. Thoughts of the night before made her shudder. I'd rather be all alone in the world than with him!

I wonder what sort of lover Poropa would have been. I think I can imagine. Just the opposite of Kedle in every way. It would not have hurt. I would have felt passion instead of pain, I'm quite positive, the way I wanted to respond to him that night at Kewa-Ma's house. She stopped her line of thought abruptly and told herself she dare not think of might-have-beens.

Finally at *big-sun* she heard a low cough outside her door. "Yes?"

Keledle-Ma, who was wife Number One, stuck her head inside the door:

"Ah, you're up."

"Yes, of course."

"I didn't want to bother you earlier in case you were sleeping."

"Oh, I've been up since dawn."

"Truly? Well, if you'll come with me I'll show you where I've put Pingi."

"*Kapogla*." Toropo gladly followed her outside and down a path which led to a little pen with a brush arbor over one corner. Pingi came quickly up to Toropo. The girl rubbed the sow behind each ear. Only the fact that the older woman was watching kept her from putting her arms around the pig's neck.

"I'm going to my garden now. I'll bring back some *kaukau* for her tonight along with some for my own pigs."

Toropo had straightened to look at the woman as she spoke.

"Thank you." She dropped her eyes back to Pingi when she noticed the woman searching her face keenly.

"You're lonely, aren't you?"

Toropo did not trust herself to speak. The sympathy in the woman's voice might start the tears. She must not cry in front of a fellow-wife.

"I'd love to have you come to the garden with me but I heard my husband tell you he'd be taking you to the mission station today. I know he's due there to check on Diye anyway."

"Diye?"

"Yes. She's Number Nine, you know. She has been in the mission *housesick*."

"Ah, yes, I heard."

"Who knows when Kedle will get around to going. He's playing cards. He could go on all night. On the other hand he could quit right now if he wins all his opponents' stakes. So you'd better stay home."

"*Kapogla*, then."

"I'll stop in and give you Pingi's food tonight."

Toropo turned to put her arms around Pingi when the woman had passed from sight, but she glimpsed a group of onlookers on the hill above her just in time. She scratched the sow's ears again instead. As she didn't know what to do while she was being watched she retraced her steps to her hut and sat down by her fire once again.

Mid-afternoon she heard Kedle's voice calling her. She hurried out.

"Let's go now."

As they were walking down the mission station driveway Toropo suddenly gasped in astonishment. Kedle half-turned back to her and then smiled understandingly as he followed her line of vision. The approaching couple was too proximate for him to speak to her then.

"*Apinun,*" he greated the young man. The two men shook hands and the younger one spoke in Pidgin.

"*Mitupela go lukim fren bilong meri bilong mi. Sarere mi kam long haus bilong yu. Yumi tupela plei kat gen.*" (We are going to my wife's friend. I'll come to your house Saturday. We will play cards again.)

Kedle nodded vigorously and the young couple passed on. Toropo studied her husband's face to see if he had understood. He probably had not caught it all, but she decided not to interpret. She wouldn't speak unless spoken to.

"What surprised you?"

"I've never seen such black skin!"

"You've never seen a Buka before?"

"A Buka?"

"That man and his wife are from Bougainville. All his people are that dark. They are called Bukas."

"Why, they are as black as Pingi!"

Kedle laughed. "Didn't you think them good looking though?"

"I didn't even notice their features. I was so surprised by their skin color."

"You look next time. That young man is a fine fellow. He and I have had many a good card game. He is one of the teachers at the mission school here. Teachers make good money, you know. He puts up a good stake."

"He works on the mission, yet he gambles?"

"Oh, yes. He's not a believer. And he never gambles on the mission station. The *kondodles* can't tell him what to do when he's off the station."

"I wonder what it would feel like to be that black."

"No different than it does to be goroka-nut-brown like you or earth-brown like me. But did you ever wonder what it feels like to be white? You would feel so pale you would be ill, I guess."

"Yes, I've often wondered that. But they're not ill, are they? Bani says some of them are very strong and energetic. I came here thinking I might see white people and instead I saw black."

"Just wait a bit. You'll see white, too."

Kedle led his new wife into the mission tradestore and bought her a pretty new *meri* blouse of bright blue, with a big red and yellow bird of paradise on it. He bought a blue *laplap*, a red one, a cooking pot, eight cups of rice, two cans of mackerel and two bars of soap. He slipped one bar of soap into his own shoulder *bilum* and handed everything else to her.

He left the store while she took time to put everything into her *bilum*. She longed to put the blouse on immediately but decided she had better not take time to find a place to do it. She hurried out and saw him approaching the big square house. As she came up beside him she saw he was heading for a window.

"You're supposed to tap on the door."

"This works fine."

He looked in the window and called, "Tamara."

A young girl whom Toropo judged to be just about her own age soon appeared at the window.

"Yes."

"Where's your mother?"

"In the other room."

"Go tell her I want to talk to her about my wife."

As the girl disappeared Toropo turned to Kedle, "She can speak like us! She talks Real-People's Talk!"

"Yes, we've taught her. A year ago she only knew a few words and sentences like a baby but now she talks well enough."

Kedle led the way to the front of the house as he heard the front door opening. The girl and her mother were waiting for him.

"Ask your mother if I can take my wife home."

Toropo listened to the girl and her mother speaking English. To her delight she recognized some words.

"She says she thinks so but perhaps we had better go ask your wife if she feels like walking that far yet."

The *ambo kondodle* was saying something else.

"*Ama* says, 'Who is this?'" the girl interpreted, squinting her nose at Toropo in Real-People fashion.

"This is Toropo, my new wife."

After her daughter interpreted Kedle's answer the *ambo kondole* spoke long and feelingly. The *bagol kondodle* hesitated in obvious embarrassment.

"What does your mother say?" prodded Kedle.

She averted her face. "She says you are wicked. Naughty! Naughty! She says you know the Bible says one man and one woman shall be one flesh, not one man and two women, or one man and ten women."

Kedle interrupted, "You tell your mother I'm too old to learn this new talk. My ears are deaf. She must teach it to the children. But what else did she say?"

"You don't want to hear."

"Tell me."

"She asks if this is why Diye let someone perform this abortion."

"Abortion! Who said anything about an abortion?"

"*Ama* knew. It was plain to see."

"By all the spirits, you're supposed to be blind."

"I know, but you asked me what she said."

"Let's go see Diye then," said Kedle, turning on his heel and leading the way to the *house-sick*.

Toropo noticed that the *bagol kondodle* kept glancing at her and smiling shyly. Toropo smiled in return. Her loneliness made her respond whole-heartedly to the girl. I'd like to get to know her, she decided. I like her eyes. But I can't read blue eyes. I don't understand what they're saying. Who could ever read cooled-off eyes? I do love her long red hair though. It covers her all around like a *purupuru*!

Kedle turned back and told Toropo to start for home. She stopped, puzzled, as loneliness swept over her once again. The *bagol kondodle* had heard and was watching her sympathetically. She raised anguished black eyes to the cooled-off ones, and they now seemed no longer cold. The girl waved and said, "*Puyo, ango*, I'll see you later."

Toropo hurried homeward, determined that they should not overtake her since they evidently did not want her company. The words, "*Puyo, ango*" kept sounding in her mind, with that slight accent.

She had been sitting by her fire for half an hour before she heard Kedle's voice. He stuck his head in the door.

"You made it home, *ltemo*." He came in and squatted by the fire, seemingly ill at ease.

"I've got a problem. I would like Diye to share our feast of fish and rice tonight. She needs good food to tempt her appetite. She isn't eating well at all and has lost a lot of weight."

Toropo waited. She determined not to help him with what he was trying to say. Finally he continued.

"Would you mind if I took a can of the fish and half the rice to her?"

"Of course not. Take it all. It's yours."

"No. It's yours. I'll only take half of it for Diye."

"Take it all. I'm not going to eat any of it. I don't want it!"

"Aw, come on, little *Konopu*, don't be difficult," pleaded the harried man.

Toropo wanted to yell that she was not his little *Konopu*. She was Poropa's. But she didn't dare.

"Won't you eat half of it?"

She refused to answer.

"Shall I come and cook it for you myself?"

No answer. He sighed and turned to the new kettle. He measured out half the rice and took one can of fish.

Toropo sat nibbling at a *kaukau* in the dusk when she heard a cough and Keledle-Ma immediately appeared at the door.

"May I come in?"

"Owiyo."

"Here is Pingi's *kaukau*." She placed a *bilum* by the door. "Oh, I see Kedle bought you a new kettle at the store. How nice!" she lifted the lid.

"Why, fish and rice! How you rate! Mind if I stay and have some too?"

"Not at all! I'd love to have you stay!"

"Shall I cook it for us then?"

"Yes, go ahead."

Keledle-Ma picked up the kettle and then stuck her head out the door and called into the darkness, "Tende-yo. Tende-*yo-eyo*."

There came an answering little boy yodel.

"Tende-yo. I'm here at the new house. Come here when you want me."

He came immediately. Why, he's just the same size as my own little Teni, thought Toropo and sighed with homesickness.

"Do you have a little brother?"

"Yes, three of them. One is just Tende's size."

"Any sisters?"

"No. My father's other wife has one daughter though, and two sons."

"But your mother has only four?"

"No, I have an older brother also."

The kettle of rice was now hanging over the fire. "Is your older brother married?"

"No, he is in his last year of high school at Ialibu."

"How interesting. Our school here at Piamble has only been going for three years. Some of our boys attended the school at Kauapena though and have gone on to Mendi and Ialibu high schools. We now have the first three grades here, and three teachers."

"I saw the Buka teacher this afternoon."

"Did you? And what did you think of him?" Tende inched closer to Toropo and was soon snuggling against her as she encircled him with her arm. When the rice was cooked Toropo ate her share, plus fish, with a surprisingly good appetite.

Keledle-Ma left her at last, towing the sleepy Tende. She detoured up around by the manhouse. Kedle sat by the fire in the big living-room area of the manhouse. He looked up quickly.

"Any success?"

"Yes, Man. She talked and cuddled Tende and ate a good helping of rice and fish."

"Woman, you amaze me."

"It was nothing."

"Now if I just knew whether or not Diye had eaten hers."

"I imagine she has. I think she's having a hard time refusing *kaukau*. She's certainly not the girl to let fish and rice set around."

"I'd appreciate it if you'd check."

"I will and ..."

"Yes?"

She wanted to ask him to leave Toropo alone tonight but that would be overstepping her mark. She had seen something akin to terror leap into the girl's eyes when she bade her good-night with the customary "sleep well." She would have liked to remind him that there were several other wives who had weaned their youngest. But that would be useless too.

"Nothing. I'll let you know if Diye hasn't eaten."

She disappeared into the night and did not return. Kedle relaxed, crawled into the bedroom beside his two older sons and slept.

Toropo woke at dawn relieved to find that she had not been visited, but had slept the night through without interruption. The hours dragged slowly by. No one appeared. "I'd love to go out but if I do the whole community will stare, or should I say, the whole family?" she asked herself wryly.

When Keledle-Ma came by that evening with Pingi's *kaukau*, Toropo's question burst from her.

"Can't I make a garden? Am I not to be given a plot of ground to work?"

"Our husband will probably assign you one next week. Why so anxious? The grind will begin soon enough. You need a little get-acquainted time first."

"Get-acquainted time!" Toropo ground out the words between clenched teeth. "I'm going to go crazy sitting here alone all day."

"Were you alone all day?"

"Yes."

"And you didn't even go out?"

"No. I don't know anyone and when everyone stares so, I can't face them."

Again Kedle left before daylight and again Toropo was grateful.

Keledle-Ma came by later to say that Kedle had said she could start a small garden just below Pingi's pen if she was that anxious to work. Next week he would show her a plot on the other side of the government road for her main garden.

Toropo thanked her. She worked long and hard all day breaking the ground with the spade Number One had lent her. She worked right up against and around Pingi's pen, often talking to the sow as she worked.

"Later, when you are used to your new home you will have to run free and find your own food, Pingi."

Grunt, grunt.

"So you had better enjoy this time of being penned up and fed your fill."

Oink, oink.

Toropo walked slowly up the path in the dusk. She wondered if she could count on having every other night to herself.

CHAPTER NINE

Just as Toropo finished the last bite of her *kaukau* preparatory to going to the garden, she heard a greeting call from outside her door.

"Yes?"

"I've come to talk to you." The voice was young and rich but unfamiliar. She was anxious to see the person to whom it belonged.

"Owiyo."

The girl (or woman?) was a real eye-catcher. Toropo gazed at the striking broad face with high cheekbones. Lively brown eyes looked back at her. The girl — no, woman, for she had a baby in the *bilum* that hung down her back — was much larger in frame than Toropo.

"Sit down, please."

The young woman smiled as she made herself comfortable on the other side of the dying fire.

"I'm one of your fellow-wives," the girl said. Her smile widened until it showed all her well formed teeth.

"Do you mind?"

"Mind what?"

"That one of your fellow-wives should come and intrude so boldly. Maybe you don't want to know us.

"Oh, my no. I do want to know you. I know there are nine of you and I want to get to know each one of you."

The girl took the baby from her *bilum* and sat him on her lap. Toropo thought instantly of *Kariyapa*. This baby was just a few months older.

"My name is Nekindi but I am already being called Jeep-Ma. This is Jeep," she said, squinting her nose down at her little son.

"Jeep? How cute! Why did you call him Jeep?"

"Because he was born in the mission jeep. I had a difficult labor and couldn't deliver so the *kondodles* put me in the jeep to take me to Ialibu Hospital. But he was born before we got there. Mrs. Talbot said all those bumps made him come."

Toropo laughed delightedly. She held her hands out to the baby.

"Jeep! Jeep! Come and see me, Jeep." The baby chuckled but sat contentedly in his mother's arms.

"What number are you?" Toropo grinned.

"I'm Number Eight" Jeep-Ma chuckled. They sat awhile in companionable silence. Toropo thought how nice it was to sit in silence with a friend again, instead of being alone.

"The reason I came was to ask if you would like to go to church with us this morning."

"Oh, really? Would Kedle let me?"

"Yes. If you go he will probably come along, though he won't go in. Many men sit outside and talk during the service."

"I see you are wearing clothes, *ltemo*. Do you always?"

"Most of the time. There are three of us wives who really believe in all the church teaches. We would like to be baptized."

"What would our husband say to that?"

"Oh, he wouldn't mind. He encourages us to go to church. He says he can see a real difference in the three of us who really believe."

"How is that?"

"We don't fight as much."

"Truly?"

"Truly."

"But he doesn't believe himself?"

"No. He says religion is for the women and children. He says he is too old and deaf to understand."

"Who are the wives who truly believe?"

"Number One and Number Six along with myself."

"And you three don't fight?"

"That's right. We don't fight."

"But you used to, before you believed?"

"Oh, I never did myself. My vices lay along other lines. But they say Number One used to be a real scrapper."

"Keledle-Ma?"

"Yes."

"That's hard to believe."

"I know. She's pretty wonderful, isn't she?"

"She is. I could love her like a mother. And Number Six?"

"They say she could hold up her end well enough in a fight at one time too."

"But you never did fight?"

"No, not here. I scrapped as well as the next when I was a child, you understand."

"You didn't feel like fighting when he married Number Nine?"

"Never! That was the day I was set free!" Jeep-Ma paused to release Jeep's fingers from the handhold he had on her hair.

"We are told when we emerge from the cocoon of childhood that life has just begun for us. My happy butterfly days didn't last long. Kedle bought me and I entered a much darker, unhappier life than childhood. So the day he married Diye I emerged for a second time. Maybe not from a cocoon, maybe it is better compared with a cave or a pit."

"You mean it? I thought wives always resented it when their husband married again."

"Most do, I guess, but not I. Being an old man's plaything wasn't my idea of living."

"An old man's plaything," Toropo repeated thoughtfully.

"Yes, half of the time you are like a *singsing* doll on display while he shows the world his newest piece of merchandise. The other half of the time you are humping it to satisfy a lecherous old man. Some people like the life, would you believe? Number Nine does. She thought she had made a great conquest when she hooked our man. She considered it a tremendous victory over eight other women. It's all in the way you look at it, you see?"

"I hadn't realized there could be more than one way of looking at it."

"Well, we will have to visit again soon. If you are going with us I'll go and inform the Old Man."

"Thank you. Is there somewhere along the way I could wash?"

"There is. I'll show you my favourite bathing spot."

Jeep-Ma hurried away to tell Kedle while Toropo gathered her soap, comb and new clothes. Then they were off to a nearby river together.

The girls washed happily in the cold mountain stream. Little Jeep was given a dunking which caused him to howl in terror.

"This is the Koglodle River, the Dead River," said Jeep-Ma.

"Dead?"

"Yes. It had a fight long ago with the Adleponga River, the Cold-Sweet River. The Cold-Sweet won."

"It did?"

"Yes. See that stone over there with the hole right through it? That was its fatal wound. Cold-Sweet speared it there. Now it's Dead."

"How interesting."

They had washed and dressed and were combing their hair when they heard a woman's yodel from the bridge.

"Ready yet?"

"Ready," they called as they hurried up the riverbank to the road.

Keledle-Ma was waiting for them with another pretty woman.

"Meet Dokta-Ma," she said to Toropo. Toropo smiled a greeting.

"She is Number Six on the marriage hierarchy," continued Number One. "And this is Dokta." She laid her hand on the slim shoulder of a little girl about five years of age. "The aidpost orderly delivered Dokta, so she was named after him."

They heard voices and looked back to see Kedle coming over the hilltop with Number Nine close at his heels. More women followed at a slight distance.

Keledle-Ma frowned and turned to Toropo. "Do you want to wait and walk with our man?"

"If you do."

"No? We'll go on then."

Toropo and her friends entered the church. The group who came with Kedle sat down outside. However most of them filed in behind Mr. Talbot when he appeared. Glancing around Toropo saw that neither Kedle nor Number Nine had come in. She could imagine her out there sitting as near to him as a woman dare sit in public. The thought needled her for some reason, but then she reprimanded herself. If I don't want him, and I don't! then why can't she have him? She turned her thoughts to the service.

Mr. and Mrs. Talbot sat at the front of the church with their four children. One boy was older than Tamara, and the other two younger, *ltemo*. Tamara and her mother each held an orphan baby on their laps.

There was also another family up front, brown-skinned and extremely good-looking. The pretty young wife sat closer to her handsome husband than Toropo had ever seen a wife sit in public. They had two darling sons.

"Who are the Real-People couple?" Toropo asked Jeep-Ma in a whisper.

"They are teachers from the coast. He is our headmaster and she teaches first grade. Their names are Joe and Janice Holowi."

Toropo could not take her eyes off Janice. She was pretty, so poised, so graceful. She reminded her some of Nancy Wembi of Kauapena but she was more dignified than Nancy. Or wasn't that the word? More genteel? More sophisticated? Toropo could not quite put her finger on the quality.

When Mr. Talbot got up to lead the singing, Tamara played an accordion. Toropo gave them her full attention. She had never seen an accordion before and she was as delighted with it as with Peter's guitar.

Toropo's thoughts strayed to Peter when the singing was over. "Some day you'll hear me calling," he had sung. Was it only a month ago? It seemed to Toropo that she had lived nearly a lifetime since then. She had been so young and carefree the day she had listened to him. Now she was an old married woman and so much wiser. That is to say, she thought ruefully, I know a lot more about men than I did then. Does that make me wiser?

Tamara and her older brother began playing an accordion and trumpet duet and once again Toropo was all attention. What marvelous music makers there are in this world. A horn! Now that is really something!

The *iye kondodle* was talking. Toropo's mind wandered. There was so much to think about. At other times she caught quite a bit of what was being said.

The service was over but Toropo delayed going outside as long as possible. She saw Tamara putting her accordion away and slipped up to her shyly.

"May I touch it?"

"*Kapogla.*"

"You look lovely in your blue *laplap* and blouse," complimented Tamara. "Come and see me sometime."

Toropo smiled wistfully.

Toropo was on her way home from the garden a month later when she heard a truck coming in the distance. She waited at the side of the road to see it pass. She had seen several trucks go by and it was a sight worth waiting for. They sped by like arrows released from their bows.

Before the truck appeared four young girls came in sight.

"Hello," called one.

"Where are you going?" the customary Imbo-Ungu greeting.

"Are you resting?" asked a third.

"No, I'm just waiting to see this truck that's coming."

"Where are all of you going?"

"We're just coming home from school."

"School?"

"Yes," they chorused.

"You mean English school? Aren't you too old to be in school?" They must have all been about her age.

"Yes, we would be too old to go to English school, but this is a special school for *wenepoma*, teenagers."

Toropo could hardly believe her ears. "Who teaches you?"

"Teddy and Tamara."

"Really? What do you learn?"

"Maths from Teddy, and Tamara teaches us reading, writing and spelling in Pidgin."

The truck had come and gone, but Toropo was more interested in the possibility of going to school.

"Truly! I wish I could go."

"Come along. They would be glad to have you."

"But I couldn't. My husband wouldn't let me."

"Why not ask him? You could still make gardens every morning. As we tell our parents, it is only for part of the afternoon."

"Oh, I'd love it. I'll think about asking him."

Toropo mused about her present life situation as she followed the trail homeward. She had met many new people. She found this stimulating and interesting. However the ugly stark reality of her relationship with her husband consumed her. It had not improved. In the beginning she had thought it might become easier with time. Now she knew it never would.

He came every night now, except when an occasional card game kept him home. Some nights he only fondled her, but this too was unbearable. Many nights she feared she would start screaming and never stop. She prayed desperately to *Kuro Kelkawe* and God. Mercifully They (or was it He? Were they One and the Same?) would make Kedle fall into his deep snoring sleep before her nerves were utterly shattered. Then she could slowly edge away from him in the darkness.

He never left before dawn any more, but stayed in her hut until she left for the garden. If she did not get away early enough she must endure the hostility of some of the wives when they arrived with his breakfast after searching for him at the manhouse.

Numbers One, Six and Eight were never unkind. Number Two and Three were indifferent. But Number Four, Five, Seven and Nine hated her. Diye never missed a chance of voicing her hostility. Extremely verbal, her cutting words left Toropo lacerated and bleeding emotionally. Even if their husband was present at her diatribes he took no notice, *ltemo*, except to say occasionally, "Now, now, we must learn to live together peaceably." Lately he only said it if she made some reply to Diye. Accordingly she felt that his quiet rebuke was for her alone. Was he absolutely deaf to all the things Number Nine said? Perhaps that odd deafness he professed in the presence of the *kondodle's* teachings also overtook him when Diye began her harassment.

She tried to avoid her in every way possible, but she could not keep her from coming to her home with his breakfast. When she started leaving for her garden earlier each morning, Number Nine began coming earlier. Toropo then began rising well before dawn so she could cook their *kaukau* and be off before her antagonist's early arrival, but that had led to another problem. In spite of her quiet, stealthy movements her husband had awakened yesterday morning.

"Why, *Konopu kogol*, it is still dark! No need to get up yet! Come!"

She had cowered in the corner, unable to move, so he had gone to her. He was unusually virile after his good night's sleep and she vowed never to let that happen again. Number Nine was the lesser of the two evils. Far better to endure her hostility than to spark off an extra love scene with her husband!

There were four bright spots in Toropo's dark life: the Saturday morning market on the *singsing* ground and the three church services a week. The latter were particularly good as her husband did not attend them. He usually went to the Saturday market with her if the Buka teacher had not shown up first for a card game. At the market she often saw Janice Holowi and Tamara Talbot. And two weeks ago she had had a real surprise there. Rami, a girl from her own Tona tribe who had married a Podlepo man the year before, had come to the market. Podlepo was only an hour's walk from Piamble. To be truthful, Toropo had forgotten Rami as they had never been close friends, but the sight of her that day had really lifted Toropo's spirits. Rami had come home with her and stayed till mid afternoon that Saturday and the next. Her mind turned now from her own problems for a minute to ponder Rami's.

Rami was seven or eight months pregnant and she was literally scared almost to death. There had been two difficult childbirths at Podlepo since she had become pregnant. The first woman had been carried to the mission nurse, who sent her, by car, to the Mendi Provincial Hospital. She died soon after arrival. The government refused to pay the return fare of any corpse. It cost them enough to get patients to the hospital. Either they would bury her body in Mendi or the tribe must get it home themselves.

The tribe dared not let her body be buried in a strange area or her spirit would surely return to eat all of them. They raised the money and brought the corpse home, but the men warned the women, "Never again!"

A month later another woman had a bad time.

"Hurry up and bear that child, woman," the men yelled. "You just want a truck ride to Mendi. Well, you're not getting it!" The woman had given birth, eventually, but the baby was stillborn and the mother had been very near death. Now, weeks later, she had still not recovered her health.

"I just know I'm going to have a hard time," predicted Rami. "What am I going to do, Toropo? I don't want to die."

Toropo thought death might be preferable to life.

When Toropo reached home she found the place unusually silent, no children playing, no women talking. She quickly put her *bilum*s in the house and went in and out among the huts in search of someone, anyone. At last she met Number Four coming out of her door. Though the woman's face did not encourage friendliness, Toropo spoke to her.

"Where is everyone?"

"Everyone has gone to see the fight at Siminji's house. He axed his stepdaughter. They say her left arm is cut right off and she is dying!"

"Are you going to Siminji's house now?"

"Yes, come along."

The victim was lying on the ground only partially conscious. The left arm was still connected to the body, but not by much. The bone had been cut. Dokta was there stuffing cotton into the wound to try to staunch the bleeding. Nausea took sudden hold of Toropo's stomach as she looked at the flesh and bone, the fat and tissue of the chubby girl's left breast laid open. She turned aside quickly only to see another young girl vomiting behind some bushes. She whirled away from her and ran to the back of the crowd. She discovered some fellow-wives sitting there and plopped down quickly beside Jeep-Ma.

"Make you sick?" asked Jeep-Ma.

Toropo raised her eyebrows in the affirmative.

"Sorry. Think about something else for a while."

The men were yelling at one another as they assembled a stretcher to carry the girl down to the road. Word had been sent for the mission jeep to come out to meet them.

"Here, man, tie those two poles together, can't you?"

"Where's the rope?"

"I just put some there. Ai, fellows, where's that vine I just put there?"

"Isn't that corner tied yet?"

"No, where's the rope? Are you all deaf?"

Nobody could hear anyone except his nearest neighbor. There were a surplus of bosses among the onlookers as well.

"Hurry up with that corner."

"Faster men, the jeep's down there waiting."

"You're all wasting your time. She's going to bleed to death anyway."

Toropo turned back to Jeep-Ma. "Where's Siminji?"

"He ran off to the bush."

"What kept him from finishing her off?"

"Kimu grabbed his axe and then some other men helped get him away from her."

"Why did he want to kill her?"

"Her mother says Siminji wanted to make the girl his wife, and she rebelled."

"He wanted to marry his stepdaughter?"

"Yes. Now he admits the only reason he married her mother five years ago was because he liked the looks of her daughter. 'Did you think I wanted an old woman like you?' he asked her mother today."

"But she would have been only a little girl then!"

"I know. Isn't it awful?"

"It's terrible."

"She has always been a chubby little thing, even years ago. I suppose that made her extra desirable."

"How come her own father's tribe let her go with the mother instead of keeping her like they usually do?"

"Her father was killed in a land fight," answered Dokta-Ma. "The tribe was small and poor from so many fights over land. Siminji drove a hard bargain paying little for her mother, saying she was 'secondhand' and refusing to take her without the daughter. The tribe was so hard-up that they agreed to it."

"For five years she has thought of him as a father," murmured Toropo. "Today she's supposed to suddenly switch her thinking. Now he's her husband, or wants to be."

"Mm," agreed Jeep-Ma.

"The poor kid."

"Either live with me … or die! Not much of a choice, was it?"

CHAPTER TEN

When Rami didn't show up at the market one Saturday Toropo took Tamara by the hand. "My husband left this morning for a big card game at Nagapo. He won't be back until tomorrow evening. Please come home with me and teach me to read Pidgin."

"*Kapogla nagol* ... if he's gone why don't you come to my house? All the materials are there."

"He said I couldn't go to school at the mission. If you come to my house he couldn't call that 'school at the mission.'"

"*Kapogla* then. Come with me while I ask my mother and get the books."

Tamara received permission. It was arranged that Teddy would come to walk her home in the late afternoon. Toropo gazed hungrily at the books and pencils in Tamara's hand. She could hardly wait to get home and get started.

"This word is Kowi and this one is Sita," began Tamara when they were seated by Toropo's fireplace. "Kowi is a boy and Sita is his sister. This says 'Book One.'"

"So book is spelled b-u-k in Pidgin. That looks funny. I'm used to b-o-o-k."

Tamara stared at Toropo. "I thought you never went to school."

"I didn't, but I always wanted to go. I learned all I could from my two brothers."

"You know the alphabet and the word 'book.' What else do you know?"

Toropo recited from memory a page of the second grade reader. Tamara listened with growing astonishment.

"And you want me to teach you Pidgin?"

"Yes, please."

"But you already know so much English. Pidgin is so easy! You'll learn it in no time since you already know the letters and can read English."

She opened the book to page four.

"This is 'I stap.' Read me this page now."

"Papa I stap. Mama I stap. Kowi I stap. Sita I stap."

"Good. Now what is this word?"

"Long."

"Yes, and this one?"

"I don't know."

"It's house. See, you can sound it out; au says the same thing as ou or ow in English. Haus."

"Oh, I see."

In no time they had finished the first primer. Pidgin was a phonetic language, Toropo discovered. Once Tamara had taught her the sounds each letter made, she thought it was great fun sounding out new words for herself. Each one seemed like a discovery, a new world conquered. She grew more and more excited. Tamara only needed to assist a little.

Toropo immediately began to devour the second primer. Some of the other wives and children came to watch them but she was so absorbed she hardly noticed. Just as she reached the last page of the second primer Keledle-Ma entered the hut with some bananas and sugar cane.

"Oh, thank you, Keledle-Ma. You're as good as my mother! I was reading and forgot that Tamara usually has a midday meal."

Toropo dug coals from the ashes and blew up a fire. They talked while they peeled *kaukau* and dried them by the flames. Once they were baking in the ashes Toropo picked up the third and last primer.

"Wouldn't you like to write for awhile instead?"

"If it's all the same to you I'd rather read. I've spent hours alone learning how to write. I can do that when you're gone. True, I don't know how to spell in Pidgin but I can learn that from these books later. Now I need you to help me with any words I can't sound out in this last, hardest book."

Their audience left when they settled down to reading again. When Toropo finished the last book she laid it aside and picked up her *koinje*, her bamboo tongs.

"Thank you for teaching me to read Pidgin, *Konopu*," she said as she withdrew the baked *kaukau*.

"Thank you for letting me teach you! It was fun for me, too. I've never taught anyone who learned this fast before. I wish you could come to my classes and show the kids a girl their age who can read."

"Everybody says *wenopoma* are too old to learn. Why do you try to teach them?"

"Because it's not fair to them if I don't. I'm a teenager myself. If I had never had a chance to learn I'd want one. Mom said if I felt that way I could teach them. Teddy helps me but he doesn't enjoy it. I'd be afraid to do it without him though."

"How old are you?"

"Fourteen."

"Bani thinks I'm about fourteen, too. He is about four years older than I. His teachers figure he is about eighteen."

"Yes. I thought we were about the same age."

The two girls sat together in friendly silence, eating their *kaukau*.

"Thank you for calling me *Konopu*," murmured Tamara. "The other girls don't. Only a few old women call me that."

Toropo studied the *bagol kondodle*. "Cooled-off eyes are hard to read, *Konopu*. But we'll be friends."

"We can't be very close friends when most of your time is taken up by your husband. He's in the way, you see."

"I know."

"What's it like to be married to an old man?"

"No good. I'd rather be dead."

"I imagined it must be pretty bad. How I wish I could help you!"

"There is no way you can help me unless you'd pray to God to strike my husband dead."

"Oh, I couldn't."

"I could and I have! You could too, if you were married to him. You could do that a lot easier than you could sleep with him!"

"Yes, that's no doubt true."

"Have you thought about what it would be like?"

"Yes."

"How come?"

"Well, since I've met you I've thought a lot about what it would be like to be in your position. I almost said your shoes."

Toropo laughed. "And before that?"

Tamara looked intently at Toropo. "I don't think you have any trouble reading blue eyes."

"I'm learning fast. Go on."

"Well …"

"Yes?"

"Your husband has told my father more than once that if he could marry a *kondodle* he wouldn't take any more wives."

"Oh, I see." Toropo chuckled. "Can we look forward to the day when you will join us?"

"Not on your life! The very idea nearly makes me vomit!"

"Exactly! And what does your father say when my husband tells him that?"

"He never lets on that he has caught the point."

"And my husband never asked him more straightforward?"

"No. Not Kedle. Other men have, but not Kedle."

"What does your father answer them?"

"He tells them there are not enough pigs in the world to buy me."

"Not enough pigs in the world …" murmured Toropo, slowly, thoughtfully. "Oh, Tamara, you lucky, lucky girl!"

"You're right, Toropo. I am very fortunate."

"I think there's a great gulf fixed between you and me like the one your father told about last Sunday, between the rich man and Abraham."

"Yes, I know."

"I suppose this gulf is just as everlasting as the one in the Bible."

"It doesn't have to be! It ought not to be! Would to God that I could do something to help change it!"

"Come, let me show you my pig." Toropo rose abruptly, putting the subject behind her, and held out one hand to Tamara. Tamara took it and they walked down the path together.

"Toropo, your hands are so fine. I was reading a book the other day about a family of fine children. The father said that all his babies were thoroughbreds. That's what you are. You're a thoroughbred. I've been thinking it all afternoon."

"What's it mean?"

"Oh, it's hard to explain. It means the best, the very best," floundered Tamara. "The best of birth, of breeding, of heritage ..."

"Would you call Janice Holowi a thoroughbred?"

"Yes! Yes, I would. You know what I mean then?"

"Yes. I've been searching for a word to describe her to myself. And you would class me with her?"

"Yes, I would. The only difference has been in your opportunities. If you had had equal chances you would be equal."

Toropo said nothing more but hugged the compliment to herself.

They stood at the pen.

"My pig's name is Pingi."

"Pingi, eh? Sooty!"

"Yes."

"She's a big one!"

"Yes. She's due to farrow any day now." Toropo began scratching Pingi and she flopped over on one side.

"... and great was the fall thereof," giggled Tamara.

"Tell me about white man's marriage customs."

It took some time to explain them. Tamara did her best. At the end Toropo turned to her with a smile.

"Not enough pigs in the world ... but he will *give you away to the man you* want to go to!"

"Right."

"I can't fathom it. Such love! For girls, for women. It's beyond me."

The time had flown by and Teddy came to collect his sister.

They had not been gone for more than half an hour when Kedle stuck his head in the doorway. Toropo was startled. She had been sitting by her fire deep in thought.

"Surprised you, didn't I'?"

"I thought you weren't coming back until tomorrow night."

"I couldn't stay away from you."

"Did you think I'd be up to no good'?"

"Possibly."

"Whatever could I do wrong?" asked Toropo, feeling guilty over her illicit 'schooling' with Tamara.

"Well, you might have been visiting, or entertaining, my son."

"Your son? But he's married."

"Ah, but his wife has a baby."

"Oh, go on, you filthy-minded old man!"

"Thank you, but I believe I'll stay."

Two evenings later Toropo could see that Pingi was ready to farrow. She had refused the food that Toropo had brought to her. The girl gathered lots of soft ferns, of the type that mother's use for babies' bottoms, and prepared to sit up with her. It was a delightful excuse for an escape from her husband. "Thank you for choosing the night instead of the day, Pingi."

He came in search of her.

"Don't you think that old sow can take care of herself?"

"Probably, but my mother tried wiping them dry immediately after they are born and she found that more of them live, that way. It helps to get them moving, makes them breathe deeper, and gets their blood walking around."

After watching the sow straining with her contractions for a time he announced, "I'm going to bed."

When Toropo didn't respond he ascended the hill and turned left in the direction of the manhouse.

Toropo sighed in relief and smiled into the darkness.

Pingi produced ten lively piglets and was feeding them contentedly when Toropo climbed the trail to her home just after midnight.

The following week Toropo had another new experience. She became a woman at last in the full sense of the word. Physically she could now claim the title which her social position had already given her.

She moved to the *kambe ulke*, the isolation hut, and decided that the discomfort of the poorer hut was easily outweighed by the fact that it was out-of-bounds for the men. It meant a whole week of freedom from her husband.

CHAPTER ELEVEN

The dark figures moving around gathering mown grass were a part of the darkness that covered the whole land and seemed to envelope Toropo's very heart and soul.

Rami! Dear Rami! She had been in labor for two days and was now nearly ready to enter the spirit world.

Just fourteen hours earlier Toropo had been standing by her hut in the semi-dawn, longing for the Tona sunrises. Here at Piamble the sun seldom rose in glory. Usually, as now, the place was covered with fog, deep thick fog. If she came out early enough she could watch the fog move up the valley. Sometimes it came in the form of rolls of cotton wool like she had seen at the clinic; billowy, roll after roll, rolling on and over one another. Other times it was gray and wispy, and yet others, gray and soupy as it had been this morning; ugly, cold, heart-chilling. It came on and on in layer after layer, whatever form it took, until it covered everything and smothered the last bit of early morning joy out of the girl who had always met the day with eager anticipation. If her life had been happy she could have easily overcome the gloom brought on by the fog, but since it was not happy and never could be again seemingly, the fog emphasized and accentuated her unhappiness.

Suddenly out of the thick gray fog came a yodel, calling, yes! calling her!

"Toropo-yo. Toropo-yo-yo."

Fear shut off the source of her blood. What could be wrong with anyone she knew or loved? Who could be calling her?

"Toropo-yo-yo."

She did her best to put a stone in her liver and managed to answer, "Yo-yo. What -iyo?"

Then came the message: "Rami and her mother-in-law are on the government road below your home. They ask for you to come and walk to the clinic with them."

She rushed in to grab her *bilum*, calling to her sleeping husband, "Kedle! Kedle! Wake up and listen! I'm off to the clinic with Rami. She needs me!"

She had flown out the door and down the trail as though her feet had wings and felt none of the heaviness that weighed on her heart.

Rami was squatting on the ground at the point where Toropo's trail met the government road. Toropo threw her arms around her friend.

"*Konopu*! Oh, my *Konopu*!"

With her friend's arm around her, Rami rose and proceeded slowly down the road.

"Ah, yes, *Konopu*, press there," she said as she pushed the girl's arm harder against her back. Toropo gripped and hugged her friend tightly.

"My pains started yesterday morning. I wanted to come to Piamble but Unjo said no. They got stronger and harder during the day. They let up a bit at dusk and I fell asleep. Then they woke me up, hurting so bad I couldn't stand it. I thought I was going to die!"

"Oh, my poor *Konopu*! Did Unjo say you could come to the clinic now?"

"No, the last thing he said before he left for the manhouse last night was that I must not go or they might send me away … Rami gasped and collapsed on the road. Unjo-Ma and Toropo squatted solicitously beside her.

"… away on a truck." Rami gasped.

"It's all right, *Konopu*. Don't talk now."

"Press hard on my back, *Konopu*."

Toropo pressed until Rami struggled awkwardly to her feet again.

"The pains have been like this all night, *Konopu*. Pain is eating me. I can't take it! Then at the hour-of-sweet-sleep my mother-in-law said, 'Let's go to Piamble.'"

Rami was panting. The hour-of-sweet-sleep, thought Toropo. Four A.M. She's been on the road two hours.

"I couldn't just let her lie there and die," said Unjo-Ma. "I told her I'd come with her. My son is being unreasonable."

They paused for Rami's contractions three more times before they reached the clinic.

"I'm afraid there is nothing I can do," said the missionary nurse after an examination. "The baby's head is pressed so tightly against the pelvis bone that there will be no moving it without instruments. Rami must go to Ialibu. If they can't help her there they will send her on to the Provincial Hospital where the doctors can do a Caesarian."

She paused while her assistant interpreted.

"But what are we going to do? We don't have a truck here today. The men went to Hagen at four this morning. There isn't another vehicle on the station."

"Never mind," Rami answered. "My husband said I absolutely could not go on to Ialibu or Mendi anyway. I came here against his wishes but I wouldn't dare get in a truck without his permission."

All morning Toropo sat with Rami.

Tamara joined them at times. Her mother checked on the suffering girl every hour. With the help of the drugs she administered, Rami was able to snatch little naps between contractions. Then fresh pain would jerk her awake and she would cry out to the *ambo kondodle*, "Don't let me die! Don't let me die!"

Unjo appeared on the scene at *big-sun*. The *ambo kondodle* began urging him to let his wife go to the Medical Sub-Centre as soon as a vehicle came.

"No. She is going to die anyway. Let her die here."

"But she may not die if she can get help. You must let her go. She will certainly die if she stays here. Dokta and I cannot deliver the child and it is definitely not going to be born without help."

"Don't let me die!" pleaded Rami with terror in her eyes.

"Just let her die," the young man commanded. "I don't have money to bring her corpse back from Mendi."

"You can't just let her die."

When the *ambo kondodle* was out of sight the man scolded his wife.

"Get up on your knees and push, you worthless woman! Of course you can't deliver that child lying flat on your back! You're just too lazy to push and you want to go for a ride in a truck."

The exhausted girl struggled onto her knees whimpering, "It's no use. I've pushed and pushed. It won't be born." Leaning forward from the kneeling position she laid her face on the woven *pitpit* platform-bed and wept.

"Stop bawling and push, woman! What do you think the women did in the days before trucks and clinics came? They went off to their little *kambe ulke* in the bush and delivered their babies all alone. They were strong. They were worthwhile women! You women nowadays just want attention."

"Many, many women died alone in the bush in those days, Son. If you don't know it you certainly ought to," his mother interrupted.

"Shut your mouth, old woman. You haven't helped her any. Let me try my way. If she's going to die anyway, let her die here. When the women died in the bush it was no worry. They were in our own territory. If I let them go trucking her off to Mendi how will I ever get her body back? Tell me that! How will I?"

Unjo and the *ambo kondodle* argued on and off for three hours, whereupon the latter threatened to report him to the government officer. Unjo relented. His wife could go if a vehicle appeared.

At four o'clock P.M. a Real-People's truck pulled into the mission driveway. Passengers got down and went into the mission trade-store. The *ambo kondodle* hurried up to the driver.

"Are you going to Ialibu?"

"Yes, I am."

"Would you take a patient to the *haus-sik* for me?"

"Who is it?"

"A woman from Podlepo."

"What's wrong with her?"

"She's in labor and can't deliver her baby."

"No, I can't take her. I have a load of passengers up the road. I'm too full. I can't take anyone else."

"Please! She's going to die if she doesn't get help. Our men would take her if they were here but they are in Hagen and won't be back till late."

"I told you I'm loaded. I can't take her, I said."

The passengers emerged from the store just then with two bags of salt. The driver called for them to hurry. He stepped on the accelerator and turned up the driveway before they were even seated.

Toropo and Tamara were standing in front of the clinic, hoping. Mondi, wife of the head pastor, had been discussing the situation with them when the *ambo kondodle* joined them and told them what the driver had said.

"He's lying," said Mondi. "He would have room for her but the other passengers he is going to pick up have roast pork to take to Ialibu. He won't take a woman in her condition on the same truck as he is carrying meat because she would contaminate the meat."

"Even if she didn't touch it?" asked Tamara.

"Yes, even if she didn't touch it. Men will not be near women who are haemorrhaging. Such women must not go near any food whatsoever."

Just then another young *ambo kondodle* Toropo had never seen came from the big square house. She was carrying a little boy.

"The driver wouldn't take Rami to Ialibu?" she asked. "I see he went in that direction."

Tamara caught Toropo's questioning glance as her mother explained the situation.

"This is Marilyn and her baby, Ronnie," she whispered to Toropo. "She is married to my oldest brother, Ronald. Ronald and Teddy both went to Hagen with my father today."

"Why haven't I seen them around?"

"Oh, they work on a station called Tongo River, on the other side of Mendi. We don't get to see them very often. They are only here for a couple days now to get supplies and some mechanical work done."

Tamara allegorized as the two girls started back to Rami. "Womanhood lies on the ground at men's feet. They walk over her never caring. But if she is in labor to bring forth a child they stop to trample her more deeply in the mud. I can't bear it, Toropo."

"And she wouldn't be in that state if man himself hadn't put the seed in her. It's no use, Tamara. When I'm with you I think maybe women could amount to something. But today I realize again that they can't. Men will never think that we are worthwhile. They will never care about us."

"But God cares, *Konopu*."

"But He doesn't do anything about it. Men rule our world. Men kill the women one way or another. If they don't kill our bodies they kill our spirits. And who is there to stop them?"

"Some day there will be a reckoning day."

"But it will be too late to help us."

The three *iye kondodle* finally arrived home after dark. After unloading, Mr. Talbot urged the onlookers to help him gather mown grass from the surrounding lawns for padding the truck bed. Toropo pondered as she gathered grass. It seems like Rami means more to these foreign men than to her own husband. What makes the difference? The question is too deep for me, but whatever the reason, I know there is no hope for us. Our men will never change.

Mrs. Talbot took a pressure lantern and three assistants to the ward to get Rami, as she was no longer able to walk. She was near death from loss of blood.

"Why don't they come?" queried Ronald when he and his father had finished forming a deep bed of grass on the back of the truck. He took his young wife's hand and they started up the path to the clinic ward. Just then his mother appeared with the lantern and three men came into sight around the corner of the ward carrying Rami. They were only managing it in the most awkward manner possible, because each was trying not to touch her more than was absolutely necessary.

Ronald evidently grasped the situation at once for he ran up to them and took Rami's body in his arms. All three carriers stepped back relieved. Toropo gasped as she realized the young man was carrying her right up against his chest. When he reached the truck he lifted her carefully over the side to his father who placed her tenderly on the bed of grass.

If womanhood had been lying in the mud at men's feet, Toropo's heart told her, it had now been lifted and set on a pedestal by the kindly act of that young man. Toropo felt like rays of warm sunshine had burst upon her sad, shivering heart. As the Imbo driver climbed up into the seat and drove off into the night, Toropo wondered if Rami had been conscious enough to realize what the young *iye kondodle* had done.

Ronald's wife walked up to him and laid her hand on his arm. Toropo searched the pretty young face in the lantern light for signs of jealousy or anger. Instead she saw the woman giving her husband a big smile. Her cooled-off eyes were shining. She is as glad about his act as I am! Toropo thought. Then she saw with a shock that there was blood on Ronald's other arm. Would he die now? Or grow weak? or become bald? lose his manliness? Would he be eaten by a woman? Toropo's consternation eased as she became aware of the young couple's lighthearted conversation.

"Hungry, honey?"

"Hungry as a bear!"

"When did you eat last?"

"We ate about eleven."

"Come on then. Your mom and I have fixed one of your favorite meals. Bet you can't guess ..."

I wonder what a bear is, thought Toropo, as they entered the big square hut.

CHAPTER TWELVE

"Whack!"

Toropo wakened instantly to the realization that someone must have hit Kedle. She opened her eyes just in time to see two burning sticks being knocked together above her. She screamed as the shower of hot coals and sparks landed on her stomach and upper legs. She had seen the gleeful, demoniacal face of Number Nine in the light of the burning wood.

In a flash she was on her feet wrestling with her assailant while another wife was biting their husband's nose and yet another was clawing and digging him. Somehow the half-dazed, half-crazed man struggled to his feet and began tearing at the faces and breasts of his two wives with his long thumbnails. The women screamed and fled out the door with Kedle hard on their heels. He actually grabbed one heel as he crawled out. The woman fell flat on her face. He jumped on top of her, pulled her hair and pummelled and clawed her.

"Bring me burning wood, Keledle!" A crowd had been drawn by the screams.

Inside, Toropo had finally managed to grab a stick from Diye and turn the hot end into her opponent's fat bare belly. Diye stumbled backwards and fell into a corner, screaming.

"Get up and get out!" hissed Toropo, pressing the wood into the woman's shoulder, and then her back. Diye scrambled heavily to her feet, dropping the second piece of wood. Toropo grabbed it up and applied one to each bare hip in front of her, aiding her departure. "I'll make you not want to sit on your lazy bottom," yelled Toropo, as, lithe and agile, she came through the door on the heels of the other.

"I'll take care of her," Kedle said, simultaneously applying hotter sticks to the woman's bare shoulders. He felt he had sufficiently scorched Number Seven. Toropo immediately sat down to pick out the embedded bits of charcoal that had burned themselves into little pockets in her flesh.

"Bring me Kewambo-Ma," Kedle commanded Keledle when he thought he had chastened Diye sufficiently.

"So Number Five was the other one," said Toropo.

She got up and went inside again to check for coals on her *pitpit* floor and walls. Then she lit a torch and made her way down to the nearest stream. She plunged into the cold water up to her neck. Her teeth soon began to chatter but her burns were infinitely soothed. They had been sheer torture.

When she could stand the cold mountain stream no longer, she climbed out and crouched on the bank, hugging her *laplap* around her shoulders. In a few minutes the burning drove her back into the water. She alternated between the water and the bank, eventually building a little fire on the bank by the aid of her smouldering torch. Gradually the burning eased. She walked home in the semi-dawn, watching the fog roll up the valleys until it covered all that lay at the foot of the great mountain.

Toropo blew up the coals which she dug from her ashes. She lay down with her back to the fire. The front of her could not bear proximity to the heat. Her thoughts were exceedingly bitter as she lay there trying to warm her back and legs. Never had anyone attacked her so violently before. She had endured many mental attacks during the four months of her married life. The physical battle on top of it was just too much. She had to run away. She had been contemplating it for some time. She'd have done it sooner if she hadn't thought Kedle would go after her. But Diye had told her something surprising recently.

"You aren't really Number Ten. I am."

"Oh?"

"Yes. You are actually Number Eleven."

"How's that?"

"Before Dokta-Ma there was another woman who was Number Six for awhile."

"What happened to her?"

"She ran away."

"And then what?"

"Nothing."

"Nothing?"

"Yes. Nothing."

"Kedle didn't go after her?"

"No."

"Surely he made her tribe return the brideprice?"

"They say he only demanded half of it back."

"Why didn't he ask for all of it? He hadn't told her to go, had he?"

"No, fish brain. I told you she ran away. I didn't say he sent her."

"Why are you talking with me if you think I'm so stupid you can't be civil?"

"I thought this was something you'd like to know. But about getting the pay back: he did originally ask for all of it back but her tribe had spent some of it, so he accepted the remaining half."

"And let her stay away?"

Diye raised her eyebrows in the affirmative.

"Why do you suppose he let her go?"

"Maybe he didn't care."

Now Toropo understood why Diye had been planting the idea of running away in her mind. They had been planning this attack then. If she ran away she would be doing just what they wanted. Whether it was what anyone else wanted or not, she would do it in a minute if she thought she could get away with it. Her mind was in a turmoil. For hours she pondered the idea, unable to sleep.

Kedle came to her door. "How do you feel, little *Konopu*?"

"I hurt. How about you?"

She raised up to look at her husband.

"*Ama! Nanga Ara-yo!*" she exclaimed. "Whatever did they do to your face?"

"They hit me across the eyes with a fence-post. Then one of them bit my nose while the other one scratched and clawed me. They must have nearly knocked me out because it was a while before I was able to get up."

"Well, I should think so! They must have been trying to kill you!"

"Yes, they admit that was their intention."

"What was their reason?"

"Because I spend too much time with you."

"Oh, I see."

Toropo eased herself into a sitting position.

"But Diye wasn't after you, was she? She was only after me."

"Yes. That's the way it was, *ltemo*."

So Diye blamed her but the other two blamed him.

"Well, the four of us are ready to go down to the *ambo kondodle* for treatment of our burns and wounds. Will you go along?"

"*Kapogla, pamili.*"

The next morning Toropo and Kedle were sitting by her fire.

"I'm going home to visit my mother," Toropo spoke suddenly. "I haven't been home yet, you know."

"Well," Kedle rubbed his scraggly gray beard thoughtfully. "It's a bad time to go. Speckled with bandages as you are, they will think you have been through a war."

"Maybe I have."

"Well, maybe so." He was still rubbing his chin. "Perhaps it's not such a bad time after all, come to think of it. Your parents would probably get wind of the fight anyway ... and since I couldn't be loving you anyhow just now ..." His voice dwindled off. "And you don't want me touching you ..."

"You're so right! I don't!"

"But I'll miss your back to sleep next to."

"There are nine other backs you could cuddle up to and maybe help save us from another attack!"

Kedle cackled merrily.

"So you want to share me, do you? Don't you know a new bride is supposed to be jealous of her husband's attention and favours?"

"I'm going to take Pingi the Second to my mother."

"Well, now." He began rubbing his scraggly chin once again. Seeing this new side of his latest bride, he was not certain how he should react. Certainly the getting-acquainted-time was over, but then on the other hand, she had been through a lot in the last thirty hours.

"Well, now, I guess that might be all right. If your parents should mention anything about reimbursements for your burns you could remind them you had brought Pingi the Second."

"Agreed."

After a short silence Kedle began rubbing his beard again. "And when would you like to go?"

"Right now. As soon as this *kaukau* is cooked."

"Oh, I say, you are in a hurry, aren't you?"

"Right."

No more was said just then. When the *kaukau* was done she removed some for herself and laid them on a banana leaf. She handed the kettle to her husband.

With care, Toropo began to dress. She slipped a blouse over her head and tied a *laplap* around her waist, gingerly tucking the ends into her *purupuru* string. This effectively hid most of the bandages except for one on her left arm and another below her left knee. She gathered up her *bilums* and *kaukau*.

This time it was Kedle who spoke abruptly. "If you aren't back by this day next week I'll be coming after you."

"Agreed." Toropo selected the largest sooty black gilt from the squirming squealing bunch of piglets. She was elated. She had not expected to be given permission to stay home a whole week.

"I'm taking your best daughter to *Ama*, Pingi. This one looks so much like you that *Ama* will think she has you back again."

Pingi grunted softly.

"She has fourteen feeding stations just like you and she even has that little false nipple between the third and fourth ones on the left side just like yours."

More answering rumbles.

Toropo slipped a rope up on Pingi the Second's right foreleg as she talked and tightened the slipknot firmly between the two little joints.

"Owa! It hurts to bend! Maybe I'm not so wise to think of walking to Tona today. It hurts worse to move today than it did yesterday.

"You're getting too thin, Pingi. Your piglets are finishing you! You eat lots while I'm gone, won't you? Jeep-Ma will feed you every night. Moglowiyo."

Toropo started down the hill. "Sti - sti - st -sti," she called to the piglet. It took some pulling but once she was out of sight of her mother's pen the piglet followed as long as Toropo talked or st - sti - ed to her constantly.

"I guess I need my head examined, Second Pingi. I shouldn't have tried to bring you along when you aren't used to being led.

Please don't be stubborn. I absolutely can't carry you in my arms. The burns you touched when I lifted you out of the pen hurt like fire. Of course if you're too stubborn I'll have to put you in my *bilum*."

Toropo stopped by the clinic. Tamara was there interpreting for her mother. Mrs. Talbot removed the pressure bandages with extreme care. In spite of all her precautions some of them were stuck fast and had to be soaked loose with warm water. Once when Toropo winced she looked up to see tears in Tamara's eyes.

"Oh, *Konopu*, I could cry for you!"

"I'm crying, too. My eyes might be the source of tears! Not so much for the present pain as for the black future still ahead. How many more times will such things happen? And worse? I tell you I'd have liked to have drowned myself that night I cooled my burns in the stream. I'd have tried it if I'd thought it would work. But the stream was quite shallow and I can swim and float too well. I've heard tell that the body saves itself of its own accord in that case. I don't know. I suppose drowning is not for me."

"Oh, *Konopu*!"

"You mustn't even think of such a thing, Toropo," said the *ambo kondodle*. "We'll pray much for you. There are other solutions. God has the answers."

"I've prayed and prayed. These are the only kind of answers I get. There is no solution."

"Have you prayed the prayer of the sinner first of all? Have you asked God to forgive your own sins?"

"Yes, but I only go on sinning."

"How do you mean?"

"I hate! I hate! I hate Kedle with my whole heart and soul!"

"God have mercy on you, my daughter," said the *ambo kondodle*, laying a soft hand on the shoulder that was not burned.

"Could you do otherwise if you were me?"

"I don't know. I don't know, daughter. Not in my own strength, certainly."

"Well, anyway," said Toropo turning to Tamara. "I'm going home for a week. For the present I'll try not to think beyond next Thursday."

"Kedle is letting you go?"
"Yes."
"Is there a clinic at Tona?" asked Mrs. Talbot.
"Yes, there is an aidpost there."
"You be sure then that you have these bandages changed every day and get three more injections of penicillin. You can't risk infection."
"*Kapogla.* Good-by *Konopu.* See you next week."
"*Puyo, Konopu.*"
"*Moglowiyo, Ango.*"

The fresh Burnalay Cream was extremely soothing. Toropo found it did not hurt her so much to move now. Half a kilometer from Piamble she put Second Pingi into her *bilum* and sped on her way homeward. She went straight to her mother's garden.

"*Ama-yo,*" she called from a little hill in sight of the garden.
"Toropo! Toropo, my daughter!"

Her mother grabbed up *Kariyapa* and came running to meet her. Teni was faster, however. He was all ready to fly into his sister's arms when she caught him by the shoulders and held him at arm's length.

"Teni! My dear little brother! How I have missed you, my little Possum! But you musn't hug me. Try not to touch me. I hurt."

Her mother ran up in time to hear the last words.

"How do you hurt? Where do you hurt, daughter? Has he beaten you?"

"No, *Ama,* I'm going to survive. Just let me hug you instead of you hugging me." Taking her mother's worried face in both of her hands she caressed her and laid her own soft cheek against her mother's rougher one.

"Little *Ama,* you look older. Have you been sick?"

"No, *nanga bagol kogol,* I'm just growing old. But tell me about yourself."

Toropo kissed *Kariyapa* who was staring at her from his mother's shoulders. "My, he has grown!"

She reached down and put her right arm around Teni's shoulders, drawing him up against the right side of her back. "You may touch me there, Little Possum. All my burns are on the front of me."

"Burns?" asked *Ama*. Standing *Kariyapa* quickly on the ground she reached for the front of her daughter's full blouse.

"*Kariyapa* can stand alone, can he? I've been gone so long!"

"My daughter! My daughter! What have they done to you?" Quick tears sprang up in *Ama's* eyes as she saw that most of Toropo's stomach, left breast and shoulder were swathed in bandages. She lifted the *laplap* and saw that bandages reached from Totopo's knees to her *purupuru* string.

"What have they done? Oh, what have they done?"

"Let's go sit down in the shade and I'll tell you all about it, but first, look what I brought you."

"A pig! A piglet!" yelled Teni who had been staring it in the eye through the netting of the *bilum*, just waiting for a chance to ask his sister about it. Toropo handed her mother the pig in the *bilum*. Her mother immediately sat down in the shade and opened the *bilum* on her lap.

"Why, it's just like Pingi! It must be Pingi's. How many did she have this time?"

"Ten again, and they're all still alive. This is the nicest gilt, so I brought her to you."

Teni grasped the rope and *Ama* set the piglet on the ground. She swung *Kariyapa* onto her shoulders.

"Let's go to my garden. I won't do any more planting. I'll just dig enough *kaukau* for tonight. Then we will go tell your father you are home."

Ama broke a stick of sugar cane and handed it to Toropo, who immediately skinned it with strong teeth and chewed it thirstily.

"*Tsingo-we*! It tastes extra good! How nice it feels to be home!"

"All right now, tell me the whole story." Two hours later they were nearing Tona. "We will go first to the manhouse, *nanga bagol kogol*, to see your father."

"You go, *Ama*, and let me go on home. I don't want to see everybody. I just want to be in your home. I can see *Ara* there."

"Okay then. Here's the key."

Teni kept hold of his sister's hand and walked with her.

Ama was deeply disturbed as she went in search of her husband. How could they have treated her little girl so cruelly? And why should Toropo not want to see everyone? Her first visit home after marriage should have been a very happy occasion. Was it just because of her physical wounds? Or were there emotional wounds as well?

Toropo settled contentedly at her mother's fireplace. Before long her father came in and sat on the opposite side.

"How good it is to see your face again, daughter, but you haven't come back to stay, have you?"

"No, *Ara*. Did you think I might be?"

"Well, I heard you had quite a battle."

"Yes, we did. Five of us did."

"They sure had the advantage over you, sneaking up on you while you were sleeping. Did you repay them as good as they gave?"

"I think Kedle did pretty well. I know I didn't hurt Diye nearly as much as she hurt me, but Kedle gave her some more."

"Fair enough."

"He is not done punishing them yet. He won't speak to them or allow them in his sight. He refuses to accept any gifts of food they want to bring or send to him. They must keep right away; can't even bring him the regular meals. That is the worst thing he can do, you know. They wanted more of his attention, not less."

"I guess a man could refuse meals from three of his wives when he has seven others to feed him."

"That's right."

"We have been having lots of trouble here. I am so weary of trouble."

"Why, what's the matter?"

"Problems with returning wives. That's why I wanted to know right away if you were thinking of staying."

"Who is it?"

"Wapi, daughter of Pora. She married Api of Orei about ten years ago. Now she has come home saying her husband sent her away because she gave birth to another girl, her third. Api has no sons at all. His first wife had two daughters so he married Wapi hoping specifically that she would give him a son."

"But what's the problem. If he roused her you don't have to return the brideprice, do you? So why fret?"

"Well, the thing is, Api turned up about three days later saying he wants her back. She refuses to go back, saying he roused her. He demands either she return or we refund the brideprice. We have held one court session after another and still do not have it settled. I am convinced he did send her away, but we still have to make Wapi go back to him. That's the only thing I know to do."

"And did you say more than one has returned."

"Yes, Ariye, Lkoraiye's daughter ran away from her husband after a beating. But hers is straightforward. She will have to return to him and that's all there is to it."

Toropo imagined what *Ara* would say if she told him she wanted to leave Kedle. In spite of the provocation he would be just as adamant with her. And Kedle had certainly not sent her away.

"I hear you brought us a pig."

"Yes, I brought *Ama* Pingi the Second, the gilt from this litter that looks the most like Pingi."

"Kedle is a wise man."

"You think so?"

"Yes, don't you?"

"I don't know."

"He is. He's a wise man. He and I understand each other perfectly."

The days passed all too swiftly for Toropo. She saw there was no opportunity of discussing her impossible situation with her family. She would have to return to her hell-on-earth and search for another way out. She tried to put it out of her mind entirely and dwell only on the present.

She spent many contented hours with each member of her family. She read her father many articles from the Pidgin newspapers Tamara had given her. He seemed to be more interested than he had ever been to anything she had had to say to him in the past.

But the one she had wanted to see most of all was not there. She had hoped that Bani would be home. Somehow she felt if there was any possible solution to her problem Bani would know it. But he had sent word to his parents that he was working on a project in Ialibu and had to complete it before he could come home for his Christmas holiday.

Toropo said good-by to her family and started back to Piamble about midafternoon. It was raining, but she had known it would be. Still she had put off going as long as possible. Better to have a few extra hours with her family and walk in the rain if necessary.

The closer she got to Piamble the slower her feet dragged through the mud. If it had not been for the promise she had elicited from her mother she thought she would have found a way to do away with herself rather than return. But *Ama* had promised to implore Bani to come and visit her for a few days before he went away to teacher's college. Somehow she must live through the days until he could come.

She stopped in at the clinic.

"You didn't have these dressed every day, did you, Toropo?"

"No. The aidpost orderly was away getting supplies most of the week. I only had them changed twice."

The *ambo kondodle* sighed. "You have infection in several places."

"I'll come every day now."

"You'd better!"

It was nearly dark when Toropo reached her own hut. She put her *bilums* inside and went on down to see Pingi. Later when she was sitting by her fire her husband entered.

"You have returned."

"I have returned."

"Did you have a nice visit?"

"*Paa-kawiyo-we!*"

"I missed you. It was a long week."

"Oh?"

"What did your parents say about your burns?"

"They expressed their sympathy."

"And what did they say about the piglet?"

"*Ara* said you are a wise man."

"Oh he did, did he? Pombo and I understand each other perfectly."

They evidently did, at that! She withdrew some *topene-pitpit* from the fire and handed it to her husband.

"Why, thank you, *Konopu kogol*! Did you bring this for me from Tona?"

"Yes."

"That means you thought of me while you were away."

"Yes, I did." No need to disillusion the poor man by telling him what sort of thoughts she had been thinking.

"How nice!"

"If you and father understand each other so well why don't you observe the in-law taboos?"

"Don't you agree that it would look silly for a man as old as I am to call your father anything but Pombo?"

Toropo winced as he spoke her father's name. How does he escape retribution from the spirits when he disregards the taboos, she wondered.

"I dispensed with all that long ago. I observed them for the first five mothers-in-law and fathers-in-law and that was enough for me."

How like you, thought the girl. You keep on taking what you want and leaving what you don't want though most people would consider that wives and in-laws go together.

"But I do my duty," he said as though he had read her thoughts. "I let you take that piglet to your parents, for instance."

"But that was my idea, remember?"

"That's true. But I wouldn't have let you go to them with all those burns without some sort of peace offering. You just saved me the problem of deciding what to send."

"Oh, I see."

Toropo removed a couple of bandages to show her husband the infection in her burns.

"How are your wounds and those of the other wives?"

"My own are healing."

"The swelling has certainly gone down."

"Yes, it has. I don't know how the three wives are doing."

"You haven't made any solicitious inquiries?"

"No, not one! I haven't spoken to them or accepted any food from them all week."

"Think it will help?"

"It should, if they aren't too stupid to learn."

Kedle began rubbing his beard. Toropo wondered what was coming.

"So you don't feel like being fondled too much yet?"

"No, actually, I don't."

"Mm. I see. But your back is all right?" He waited for a response.

"Isn't it?"

"Yes."

Toropo survived that night and the next, though somehow they seemed so much worse than before she went away. To her great delight she met Rami at the market Saturday morning.

"You're alive and well!"

"Yes, thank God."

"But the baby?"

"My baby boy died."

"Sorry, *Ango*. Tell me about it."

"They delivered him with instruments at Ialibu but he was too weak to live. He took a few breaths but he never even cried. They worked with him but it was no use."

"I'm so sorry, *Konopu*."

"So am I, but I am thankful to be alive myself. I'm coming back here tomorrow to go to church."

"You are?"

"Yes. I felt God in that place that night I was so close to death so I'm coming to church here to learn more about Him."

"You felt God?"

"Yes."

"How … what was it like?"

"It was heavenly."

"Heavenly? How does heavenly feel? All I know is hell-on-earth."

"Sorry, *Konopu*. I heard about it. Your burns aren't healed yet?"

"No, several are infected. I have to go get my bandages changed now. Come along with me to the clinic so we can talk some more."

The two girls walked off, hand in hand. "I've been wanting to ask you …"

CHAPTER THIRTEEN

Toropo hurried down the road as fast as she could without appearing to be running. She kept checking behind her guiltily but no one was following. In less than an hour she had reached Rami's house without being seen. All the women were at their gardens on this bright Monday morning. Toropo found her friend's house easily though she had never been in this area before. Rami's directions were explicit, *ltemo*.

Toropo coughed. Rami's head popped through the doorway.

"You're here then," sighed Toropo.

"Of course. I promised you I would be."

"I know. It's just that I'm nervous. I'm not used to sneaking."

"Anyone see you?"

"I don't think so. I walked through the *pitpit* until I got well away from home. When I did go out on the road I kept watching both ways. I went off and hid in the *pitpit* two more times while people passed by."

"Come on in so you can hide easier if anyone comes."

"Do you expect someone?"

"No, but there is always the possibility."

"When will Unjo be home?"

"Tomorrow evening if all goes well."

"Have you decided yet to tell him the truth or are you just going to let him think I'm visiting?"

"No, I haven't decided yet. I'm afraid he will let the possum out of the trap if we pretend you are visiting, but as I said Saturday, I don't know if we can depend on him to be on our side."

"I wish there was somewhere farther to go. I don't feel safe this close to home. It didn't even take me an hour to get here."

"We will have to think on it. Unjo has a sister who married a Kagodle man. Maybe my mother-in-law would consent to us going to visit her."

"How far is that?"

"It's a full morning's walk straight across the Western Highlands border. How soon do you suppose you'll be missed?"

"Probably not before late afternoon anyway."

"That's when you usually come home from the garden?"

"Yes, though I have stayed out till dark a few times."

"Would he go to Tona looking for you after dark?"

"I don't think so. I've never known him to be out after dark for anything but a card game."

"Then you are safe here for two days."

"Yes, he probably won't go to Tona until tomorrow morning."

They waited until Unjo got home the next evening. They told him everything and asked his permission to go to Napogla. Toropo was so nervous she couldn't sleep that night. They left before daylight. Napogla was lovely in the noonday sun, situated right along the Kaugel River. Toropo felt greatly relieved. She relaxed and enjoyed swimming, fishing and even frog-hunting by night. It reminded her of the days of her youth!

She refused to dwell on the future, until she looked up to see Keledle standing at the door of Unjo's sister's home one afternoon three days after their arrival.

"How did you find me?" she asked with surprising calm. She realized now she had known she'd be found.

"It's been a long search."

Toropo felt incapable of movement.

"Well, come along, woman. *Ara's* waiting."

"Where?"

"At Unjo's house."

They walked silently through the rain until darkness fell. Toropo stopped. Keledle turned around.

"Why stop?"

"I can't go on."

"You had better unless you want me to pull you or push you or drag you."

"I'd rather die than go home."

"Is it that bad?"

"Worse than death."

"It will be worse yet after having run away."

"I don't think it could be."

"Wait and see."

Keledle reached for her in the darkness. At his touch she jumped away.

"Don't touch me."

"Touchy as a cassowary, are you? Come on, then." Keledle yodelled to his father at Unjo's turn-off.

"*Ara-yo. Ara-yo-iyo-iyo.*"

"*Yo-iyo.*"

"We're here-*iyo.*"

Kedle soon joined them.

"Where was she?"

"At Napogla."

"Give you any trouble?"

"No."

For a time only their footsteps could be heard in the darkness. Kedle cursed when he stubbed his toe on a stone.

"Why did you do it?"

No answer.

"I asked you why you ran away!"

Still no answer. Kedle turned around and swung at her. He judged accurately. The slap rang out in the stillness.

"Listen, woman, it isn't wise to make me any angrier. I'm weary. Old man that I am, I walked all the way to Ialibu and back for you."

"Ialibu?" Toropo was startled out of her silence.

"Yes, Ialibu."

She wanted to ask why but decided against it. Eventually he continued.

"Yes, Ialibu, and the road's not growing any shorter I can tell you. But your parents thought you might possibly have gone there to see your brother. We were not leaving any trail untried in the search."

"Did you see Bani?" She couldn't help asking.

"I did."

"And I went to Kumunge looking for you," put in Keledle. "Poropa has gone back to work on a plantation on the other side of Hagen in case you are interested."

Imagine them thinking I would run away to Kumunge, she thought. Do they think I'm some sort of rubbish *meri*?

"Did someone put it into your mind to run away?" asked Kedle.

No answer.

"You'd better answer or I'll be tempted to beat you here instead of waiting until we get home. Let me warn you, woman, you might not feel like walking when I get through."

"I had thought of running away myself."

"But someone encouraged you?"

"Mm."

"Who was it?"

No answer.

"Was it Diye?"

"Mm."

"You ought to know better than to listen to the prattling of a jealous fellow-wife."

Kedle continued to pursue the subject some time later.

"What did Diye say to make you think it would succeed?"

"That you let the first Number Six go."

"I figured. But what made you think I would let you go? Have I ever acted like I wasn't interested in you?"

"No."

"Well, why then?"

Instead of leading her to her own house he took her to the house of Number Two where he had a club ready. There followed the thud of club on flesh and the crack of club on bone. A crowd of family members soon gathered in spite of the hour and the weather.

Toropo lay crumpled at his feet in the mud, wishing he would kill her. She knew it was not to be however. He wanted her alive.

He beat her until he was too spent to raise the club one more time.

"When she feels like talking, Toringi-Ma, tell her what will happen if she runs away again. And don't let her out of your sight until I say you may."

When he was gone Keledle-Ma and Toringi-Ma carried her into the latter's hut and placed her gently by the fire.

Two nights later the two women were lying on either side of the fire when Toropo spoke for the first time. Toringi was asleep in one corner.

"What will happen if I run away again?"

"Do you really want to know?" asked that flat, lifeless voice.

"Yes."

"The same thing that happened to me."

"So that's why he asks you to tell me?"

"Yes."

Many minutes passed before the woman began the story with obvious effort and long pauses.

"I was young and life had seemed good ... until I was married. Keledle-Ma didn't want another woman around to share her home and her husband. She would beat me and I would run away to my mother. Kedle would come and get me and beat me for running away. At last my father began to beat me for returning home and causing them trouble. He was afraid Kedle would give up on me and demand he return the brideprice. So that last time I ran away to the village of my cousin and her husband. She had been my best friend before we were both married. It took Kedle some time to find me ... and when he did ... he gave me ..."

The pauses were getting so long Toropo wondered if she wouldn't continue.

"... the famous tribal punishment for run-away wives."

"Tribal punishment?"

Toropo began to wonder if the woman had fallen asleep.

"You never heard of the ... tribal punishment?"

"No."

"You're so young ... and innocent."

"Not any more. I'm getting old and wise."

"The tribal punishment ... is when ... every man in the tribe ... lies with you."

Toropo stared at her uncomprehendingly at first.

"All at once?"

"One after another."

"*Ama, nanga Ara-yo!*"

There was a long silence during which Toropo groaned aloud two different times as more complete realization dawned upon her.

"Kedle's tribe is a big one ..."

"Very big indeed ... when you number the men that way."

"*Ama, nanga Ara-yo!*"

"My heart and liver died that day ... They drowned in shame and humiliation. I have never looked any man in the eyes ...

since ... and very few women. Only my body lives. I never go anywhere ... except to the garden and back."

Toropo now understood why the woman had no life in her voice.

"I have never enjoyed anything since ... I seem to have no ability to take pleasure in anything. I loved my babies. I had two girls. One was married a few years ago. I loved them ... I cared for them ... but I can't say I ever enjoyed them. I don't know if I could have, if they had been boys or not. I could only think of the sadness that would come in their lives ... I could only fear for them."

Toropo groaned in sympathy.

"As I said, only my body lives ... but it lives well somehow. It is strong. When I get sick I never go drink medicine but somehow I always get well again. I have pleaded with the Good Spirit and with the bad ones too ... to take my life ... but I live on."

"Toringi is such a lovely child," said Toropo slowly. "She is my favourite of all Kedle's children. I never could understand where she got her vibrancy and her love of life."

"She is like I was before I died. It is dangerous to be so vibrant, so in love with life. The more capacity you have for enjoyment the deeper your capacity is for suffering as well. I had hoped to teach my daughters ... a stoicism that would shield them from suffering. I think I succeeded in part with my older daughter, but with Toringi I have failed utterly."

"The way she loves school and loves learning reminds me of my own self at her age. Did you know she often came to visit me, when I had my own house, to share the things she was learning with me?"

"Yes. She has told me you were interested."

The two women slept at last.

"Do you think you might be well enough to go to the garden today?"

"To your garden?"

"Yes. I am not supposed to leave you so I didn't go these past two days but perhaps we could go this morning. I could fix you a shady place to rest nearby if you want to lie down during the day."

"*Kapogla. Pamili.*"

It became a daily pattern. Toropo, Toringi and her mother went to the garden together each morning, came back together each evening, fed the pigs together, did everything together.

School was out for the summer holidays so Toringi became Toropo's shadow. Toropo learned to love the little girl more and more. I could not love her more if she were my own sister, born of my own mother, she thought. Both of them had keen minds and though Toringi was only nine or ten years old they had long stimulating conversations together. Toringi had just completed the third grade and she often thought of some new English word to teach Toropo. They talked together in halting English, laughing over their own and each other's mistakes. Toropo taught Toringi to read her Pidgin books and newspapers.

Toringi's mother watched over them fondly but with fear in her heart.

Kedle could not stay away from Toropo for two weeks though he had meant to punish her longer by snubbing her. He soon realized however that she preferred his absence. He was only denying himself. That night and often thereafter he went to her at the home of his second wife.

Toropo was deeply humiliated. His attentions in the privacy of her own home had been unbearable. There were not words to describe her repulsion and humiliation at having to receive him in another's house. Though the darkness kindly hid them, it could not dull the sounds.

"God, have mercy!" she pleaded again and again. Her hatred grew in her until it became a cancer consuming both body and soul. Nevertheless it was at this time that she conceived.

The only outlet she had for her disturbed emotions was digging the ground and forming the *kaukau mundus* next to Toringi-Ma. She dug and poked, beat and pummeled the ground as though it were Kedle's flesh under her fingers or spade or digging stick.

"The girl works like one possessed," Toringi-Ma told Keledle-Ma. "Kedle is going to have to give me a larger plot of ground. We have finished all that he gave me and her too. She even clears and breaks new ground like a man."

"She never voices her anger and hatred," said Keledle-Ma. "She only allows them expression in the form of work. I fear for her."

"So do I. I have come to love her like a daughter. I wish I didn't for I know it will only mean cause for fresh suffering."

"When one is human one cannot help loving. And until woman becomes a spirit there will always be suffering for her. You can avoid neither, my Sister."

CHAPTER FOURTEEN

Toropo raised up from her *kaukau* mundu to look straight into the eyes of her brother.

"Bani! Bani" she screamed and flew straight at him, unheeding the spoiling of her carefully shaped *mundus*. She was in his arms laughing and crying at the same time.

"My brother, my brother! Oh my brother, you have come to me at last!"

"I have come, Little Sister, I have come." He held her for a long time, wondering much at her tears and laughter. Never had his coming put *anyone* into such happy hysterics before.

That afternoon Toropo approached the manhouse of her own accord for the very first time. Kedle looked up in surprise.

"My brother has come. May I return to sleep in my own house and entertain him there?"

Kedle rubbed his scraggly beard.

"I don't know if I can trust you."

"You can."

"How do I know I can ? How can I believe you?"

"I promise you that I will never run away again."

"I'm an old man. Too old to be chasing run-away wives."

"If I run away again you can kill me."

"Ha! Kill you? I think you would have liked me to kill you this time. That gives me no assurance you won't run away again."

Toropo had looked him straight in the eye when she made her promise. Now she dropped her head and said in a throaty voice, "I heard Toringi-Ma's story. I vowed I'd never run away again."

"Oh, you did, did you? You would fear that more than you would fear death." Kedle cackled delightedly. "Thank you for letting me know. I'll keep it in mind. Yes, you may return to your own home. Give your brother my greetings." He reached behind him. "And here. Here's a nut for the girl I love."

"Thank you," said Toropo, slipping the big cloven half of pandanus nut into her *bilum*. She returned to Toringi-Ma's house where Bani waited.

"He says I may, Bani. Your coming is a double blessing."

She turned to Toringi-Ma.

"He gave me my freedom, *Ama*. I may return to my own house."

"I shall miss you, daughter."

"Truly?"

"Truly."

"Then I shall come again often to see you and my little sister. Thank you for all your kindness." She stooped down suddenly and kissed the leathery cheek. To her surprise she saw quick tears spring into the sad old eyes.

Bani helped her gather her *bilums* and belongings and carry them to the small hut on the far side of the family hill. Toropo greatly enjoyed serving her brother the nut and other foods. They talked into the night.

"… and how do the other wives react?"

"In different ways. I think there are as many different reactions as there are wives."

"Tell me about them."

"Number One goes on loving him, it seems, striving to please him, never resenting anything he does. She is an amazing woman, truly!

"Number Two, whom you met, seems completely indifferent. It seems like she doesn't feel anything toward him. I had often wondered about her and now I know her story. She received a terrible punishment for running away when she was young. She says her heart and liver died then. Only her body lives on. She never goes anywhere but to her garden. She looks a lot older than Keledle-Ma but she is really younger.

"Number Three is an old woman. She had had three children before she married Kedle. Her husband was killed in a tribal war. She asks for nothing and seems content with a tenth of a husband to call her own.

"Number Four is different. I thought she didn't like me at first but I just didn't know her. She is all wrapped up in her children. She has a son. Can you believe this? Kedle only has four sons even though he has ten wives! Imagine that! Number One

has two sons, and no daughters. Number Four has one son and one daughter. Number Eight has a baby boy. *Ara* has two wives and six living sons. *Ama* alone has had five sons!"
    "*Ara* now has three wives."
    "Three?"
    "Yes, three."
    "Why, when did he take a third one?"
    "Three weeks ago."
    "*Ama-yo*! I wonder if it had been already arranged when I was home."
    "It was."
    "But *Ama* never mentioned it."
    "No? I suppose she thought you had enough troubles of your own."
    "I really thought she had aged. I asked her if she had been sick."
    "Yes, it has really aged her. Either that, or her concern for you. I don't know. She has just sort of given up; let herself slide into old womanhood or whatever you'd call it."
    "She didn't fight it?"
    "No, but she sure would like to fight your cause for you if she could. She is terribly concerned about you. Are your burns all healed?"
    "Yes. Two of them got worse after my beating but they are healed now."
    Toropo cracked a roasted nut between her strong teeth.
    "What is the new wife like?"
    "Oh, all right, I guess."
    "Describe her to me."
    "Well, she is a little older than you. A lot fatter. Not nearly as pretty as you."
    "How did Mombo-Ma take it?"
    "Not so good."
    "Do they fight?"
    "Yes. Both with words and with more substantial weapons."
    "Owa. I'm glad I'm not there then."
    "Yes. It's not pleasant to be around. I'm glad I'm due to go to Teacher's College next week. But tell me about the other wives. You only got to Number Four."

"Oh, yes. Well, Number Four is all wrapped up in her son, as I said.

"Then Number Five is resentful. She hates being an old wife, five-times-replaced already. She is still young and attractive. She has only one child who has been weaned long since. She would like another, I know.

"Number Six is a lovely woman. Happy and kind. I like her a lot. She doesn't seem to resent Kedle's lack of attention though her only daughter has also been weaned for some time.

"Number Seven hates me although she never says anything much to me. Neither did she try to hurt me that night she and Number Five clobbered Kedle. They just took their feelings out on him. She has a little daughter still nursing. She *eye-greases* Kedle's son, Keledle, a lot. I rather think he may like her too.

"Then there's Number Eight. She's a delightful person. Her little son is just walking now. She never liked Kedle it seems, and she was happy when he got another wife. That was her dancing day! She is supposed to be a Christian, but she is having a flirtation with one of the pastors down at the mission station. When I remonstrated with her she said, 'Oh, don't worry. It's just a harmless flirtation. We won't let it go too far. After all, he's a pastor. Besides, I have my little Jeep to nurse. I wouldn't do anything to jeopardize his progress. It's just that it's important to me to prove to myself that I can attract someone besides our lecherous old man.

"Number Nine loves Kedle with a very jealous love and she hates me with her whole heart. She was the one who burned me, you know. Also she told me about the original Number Six who ran away and was let go. She helped me think it might be possible for me to run away." Toropo paused thoughtfully. "No, that's not really true. In my heart I knew it wasn't possible. I tried it simply because I was desperate."

"Why does she hate you and love him? It's not your fault you're here. It's his."

"She hates me for living! She hates me for breathing! She hated me the day of the *singsing* before I even knew who Kedle was."

"And you're terribly unhappy? You don't feel you will ever be able to reconcile yourself to this marriage?"

"No, never. I'd rather be dead."

"Now that *Ara* has bought another wife he couldn't return the brideprice even if you left Kedle."

"No. If I left Kedle *Ara* would just make me return. He would have even before he bought this other girl. You know him. That's why I didn't go home when I ran away."

"Oh, Sister, I don't know what you can do. Who can we talk to about it?"

"I've just been waiting to talk to you, hoping you'd have a solution."

"But where will I find the solution, *Aya*? My, what a mess! I believe I had better marry only one wife and stick to her for life the way the teachers and missionaries do. It would avoid all these problems."

"And don't sell your daughters when they grow up."

"Don't sell my daughters?"

"No. Let them marry who they will. If you want a brideprice you'll have to get the most you can. Your daughters will end up in the same mess I'm in because the old men have the most to offer. They've had longest to get rich."

"But it's our custom to accept brideprice, *Aya*. That can't be changed."

"Not everyone does."

"Why, what do you mean?"

"Tamara says Joe Holowi, the Piamble Community School Headmaster, did not pay a brideprice for his wife."

"Where is he from?"

"He's from Manus. She's from Morobe Province."

"And he didn't pay for her?"

"No."

"What is she like?"

"You are wondering if she wasn't worth payment?" chuckled Toropo. "No, there's nothing wrong with her. Her eyes aren't crossed. Her legs are the same length. She's not deaf, lame or blind. What's more, she's beautiful. And she's also intelligent and educated. She is a teacher."

"That's hard to believe. All the coastal people I know pay for their wives. In fact, coastal girls are *dia tumas*. They cost more than our highland girls — sometimes thousands of *kina*!"

"Thousands?"

"Yes, fathers of educated girls say the husband will soon get it paid back to him because their daughters can teach, nurse, act as stewardesses, secretaries and whatever. So they charge thousands."

"But Janice is educated. I wonder why her father didn't charge thousands for her."

"She didn't *go nothing* to him, did she?"

"Of course not. Janice is not a whore! She's the very opposite of a low woman in every way, Bani. She's sweet and a little shy, very feminine and graceful. Tamara called her a thoroughbred. Have you heard that word?"

"I've read about thoroughbred horses."

"Yes, that's it. Tamara said it was the best of race and breeding."

"Maybe we ought to talk to the Holowis, then, *Aya*. We could tell them of your problem."

"Why, I never thought of that." She rearranged some half-burned sticks of wood to make them burn better. "But I'd be afraid to go to their house, Bani. I've only ever talked to Janice at the market. I'd rather go to Tamara's house than Janice's, and that's scary enough."

"Nonsense, I'm not afraid. I'll get permission for you tomorrow from Kedle and we'll go to see them."

He began to chuckle.

"What's funny?"

"I'm more afraid to ask Kedle's permission than I am to approach Mr. Holowi."

"Really?" Toropo laughed too. "Never mind. I'll ask him. I'm not afraid when you're here."

"*Kapogla*," said Kedle. "I don't mind if you visit the Holowis, but you don't want to miss the courts, do you?"

"Oh, the courts! I'd forgotten about them. I'll tell Bani."

"Bani, I forgot that today is a special court day. The *kiap* will be coming out to settle a sorcery case about Kogla's death and some other matters. Kedle's just gone. Shall we go too?"

"*Kapogla*. Which *kiap* is coming out from Ialibu?"

"I don't know. Are there more than one?"

"There are three."

The *kiap* was seated behind a table in a small brush arbor.

"Shut up! Shut up!" he bawled.

The crowd fell silent.

"Let's take up the smaller matters first. Once we get started on that sorcery case we'll be here till dark."

Village magistrates immediately brought forward two men.

"He built his store on my land," began one.

"It isn't his land," countered the other. "It belonged to my grandfather. My own father had gardens on that very spot so, of course, the land belongs to me."

"No, my father let his father use that ground for his gardens because one of his wives had swollen joints and couldn't walk far. This plot was close to their house. But my father never gave him rights to the land and since he wouldn't listen to me we chopped his store with axes."

Two hours passed as the patrol officer listened to land disputes, minor theft cases and an adultery case. Tamara had joined Toropo and been introduced to Bani. They chattered together in low tones until their attention was caught by a new case. An old man named Odle was complaining that one of his wives would not obey him. She would not make gardens. She was lazy.

"Well, what am I supposed to do about that?" yelled the exasperated white man. "Beat the jolly woman! Slap her up. Make her listen to you. Aren't you the man in your own house? Don't you wear the pants, I mean the leaves?"

The crowd laughed uproariously. Odle stood silent, sheepishly waiting for the laughter to subside.

"You want me to beat her, do you? Yes, I'm the man in my own home. I killed a wife once ago and I could just as easily kill this one. It's a bit of waste but ..."

"Stop! Stop! I didn't mean kill her!" The Australian was aghast. "Can't you men find a happy medium? I just meant slap her up a bit. Let her know who's boss. I don't mean kill her." He swore. "Of course you can't kill her. Why, we have a man in the *kalabus* right now that I wish we could hang for killing his wife."

The crowd gasped when this was interpreted.

"He deserves it!" continued the patrol officer. "He chopped her in two right in front of our office in Ialibu. He told everyone that he is not afraid of the government or the jail, so I wish we could hang him. We've got to do something to show you men you can't kill your wives!"

The man shook his big red head vehemently. "No, no, when I say 'Show 'em who's boss' I don't mean kill 'em." Another curse. "How can a dead woman learn who's boss?"

Toropo turned to Tamara. "So white men don't kill their wives but they beat the jolly woman 'to show 'em who's boss,' do they?"

Tamara blushed. "Some of them do evidently."

"That's not like your father, though."

"No, it's not like my father or any men I know. But there are lots of bad white men, Toropo, very bad. Newspapers in America are full of the deeds of wicked men, white men! American men don't buy their wives or sell their daughters but that doesn't mean they all treat women nicely!"

"Maybe not all white women deserve nice treatment either," put in Bani. "Maybe there are some lazy white women just like Odle's wife here."

"Yes, there are. I know some. There's all kinds in any skin color."

"I just can't picture a white man acting like that. When I think of a white man I think of your father, or your brother who carried Rami."

"Just look at the one sitting in front of us."

"Do you suppose the *kiap* beats his wife?"

"I don't have any idea, except that he seems to think it's a natural solution. 'Beat the jolly woman. Slap her up!' As though it's something you'd do any day of the week!"

"Do you know him, Bani? Does he beat his wife?"

"He's not married."

"Not married! *Aminienga glapa!* Why he's old enough to be a grandfather! Why isn't he married ?"

"I don't know," said Bani.

"Maybe he's just a bachelor," said Tamara.

"What's a bachelor?"

"Someone who never married, or doesn't want to marry."

"But when your women are free why would any man not marry? We don't have any bach —, whatever you call them and our men have to buy their wives."

"Maybe no woman wanted him."

"Do you suppose?" Toropo turned to look the big *kondodle* over well.

"Or maybe they just don't want to marry."

"What sort of man would not want to marry? Imagine growing old without children."

"But what man wouldn't want sons? And who will take care of him when he gets old?"

"There are homes, institutions, for the old people, Toropo, but I don't think that's a satisfactory solution. It's nicer the way you Real-People take care of your old grandmothers and grandfathers."

"But what sort of man wouldn't want to marry?"

"There are women in our countries that never marry either."

"Oh, *Konopu*, you must be joking."

"No, I'm serious. It's true."

"What's wrong with them?"

"Nothing, probably. Some never get the chance. Others don't want to."

"What do you mean they never get a chance?"

"No man ever asks them to marry him."

"*Aminienga glapa*! I don't like that idea!" Toropo pondered. "Never being asked would be as bad as being married to someone you don't like."

"Yes, it might be," agreed Tamara.

"Here come the Holowis, Bani. Tamara, would you introduce Bani to them?"

Tamara would and did.

"Glad to meet you, Bani," said Joe Holowi, extending his hand.

"My sister tells me you're the headmaster here."

"That's right. And what about you? Are you still in school or already working?"

"I just graduated from Ialibu High School. I'm going on to Goroka Teacher's College next week."

"That's great. Let's sit over here in the shade and talk. We have fifty minutes before school resumes."

"How do you like Piamble?"

"Oh, it's a little too cold and foggy for my liking but at least there is plenty of cheap firewood."

"There is that!" agreed Bani, eyeing the wooded steeps of Mt. Giluwe.

"And you're from Manus?"

"Yes. I'm from Manus. It's a good deal warmer there."

"I guess so. From a coastal island to the foot of the second highest mountain in P.N.G.! What do you miss most about Manus?"

"Other than the family I suppose I miss diving and spear fishing the most. But … . "

Joe paused and everyone looked up at two young men who walked by them conversing animatedly. "… and so he wishes they could hang him."

"Who do you suppose they are talking about?" Joe asked Bani.

"A man in Ialibu who killed his wife."

"Really? Did you know the couple?"

"I knew her because she worked in the Outpatients Department of the hospital. I saw him once or twice."

"What was he like?"

"An oldish fellow, short, thin, gray."

"And she?"

"She was young and beautiful. She had the prettiest eyes. She didn't talk much with her mouth but those eyes talked all the time. Young men were just crazy about her."

"And what happened? Tell us all about it."

"Well, the old fellow heard that she was seeing some young man. He promised her if it happened again he would kill her."

"And it did?"

"It may have. Anyway he thought so. He chased her with an axe all the way from their home to the government office."

"I suppose she kept running, thinking if she could make it to the office she'd be safe," shivered Tamara.

"Yes, he could have killed her anywhere along the way but he wanted to do it in front of the office. To show the patrol officers. One of the officer's wives was a special friend of the girl and the old codger wanted to show them he still had control over her even if she was a nurse and working for the government!"

"*Ama, nanga Ara-yo!*" groaned Toropo.

"He said he wasn't afraid of jail or anything. He chopped her right in two. I saw her myself. She was lying face down split right in half, each side of her lying open to view. You could see all her organs. It was such a shock. I had seen her just the day before at Outpatients, so much alive! And there she was laid out like that. I'll never forget it."

"Oh, men, men! How can they be the way they are?" moaned Toropo.

Janice turned to Toropo. "I hear you had some pretty rough treatment while we were on holiday. Is that true?"

Toropo raised her eyebrows.

"Did you hear about the women burning her and Kedle beating her?" asked Bani.

Joe and Janice nodded. "Not much fun being the tenth wife of a *lapun*! I can imagine," stated Janice. "Are you terribly unhappy?"

"I'd rather be dead."

"I hate to go off to Goroka and leave her here in such a situation. Who can tell what might happen next?"

"But your father wouldn't let her return home?" Joe asked Bani.

"No, he wouldn't. You see, Kedle paid a tremendous amount for Toropo and *Ara* has already used the bridewealth. He bought wives for two of my cousins as well as buying a third wife for himself."

"Mm," from Joe.

"And it's no use running away?" from Janice.

"No, it's not. I'll never run away again," said Toropo.

"Why don't you tell the patrol officer your story while he's here?" asked Joe. "Find out what he suggests."

"Oh, I couldn't. I'd be too scared. My husband is here." Toropo remembered an old custom of unmentionable things being done to the wife who dared to take her husband to court.

"What could he say," asked Bani, "besides telling her to return home and have our father refund the brideprice?"

"I don't know but at least she could complain about her unfair treatment, the burning and the beating."

"A village court would say she had no claim. Kedle gave our parents a piglet when she was burned. And a beating is just punishment for running away."

"So everything's even?" asked Joe, shaking his head. "But it's not. There's a double standard here, Bani, that's not right.

Just like that girl you saw chopped in two. How many women had that old codger had already in his lifetime? But the girl is supposed to be content with an old man and not even look at a young one. Do and you'll die!"

"Mind if I ask a personal question?" asked Bani.

"No, I don't think so. Go ahead."

"Is it true that you didn't pay a brideprice for Janice, or is that just a rumour?"

"It's true." Joe glanced at Janice with a little smile.

"But that is unusual? Even on the coast?"

"Yes, it is. You see, Janice's father is the pastor of a Lutheran Church. He feels it is wrong to sell his daughters. He would not take one *toea* for her. Not even a gift. My brothers and uncles tried to give a gift to Janice herself, but her father would not allow her to accept it. He realized it was in lieu of the brideprice."

"Is this the solution?"

"I don't know, Bani. For us, it's all right. As long as we live away from my tribe. There are so many ins and outs to the question; so many implications. I'm not one bit in favour of inflated brideprices. I think a token brideprice might be the solution myself."

"What do you mean by a token brideprice?"

"A token payment. An amount easily within the means of all young men. Perhaps one or two hundred *kina* which would be the equivalent of the usual traditional bridewealth value. This could be the seal of the marriage and yet an unhappy wife could find it to refund herself, rather than choosing suicide as the only way out."

"Then there'd be a lot more divorce."

"Yes, and that's not good either. But it may be the lesser of the two evils. There would be fewer suicides and fewer unhappy women in our land."

"But for the present, what can we do for Toropo?"

"I don't know but if she were my sister I'd do something!"

"What?"

"I would go to the patrol officer myself, if need be."

"You don't know our father."

CHAPTER FIFTEEN

"Here are four of Kedle's wives. Let me introduce them to you. This is Keledle-Ma. She is Number One. This is Dokta-Ma, Number Six. That one is Jeep-Ma, Number Eight. And this is Toropo, his most recent addition, Number Ten. Over there are two others." The woman called to them. "Diye! Diye-yo! Kewambo-Ma! Come on over here! I want you to meet my new daughter-in-law."

Both women got slowly to their feet and sauntered over. It was Saturday morning. Market was over. Kedle was off to Marapugul, on the Kaugel River, making negotiations to buy exotic bird feathers. He had left yesterday morning and was to be gone three days.

Toropo watched Rare-Ma and her new daughter-in-law with interest. What would it be like to have a mother-in-law? I wonder how many years ago Kedle's mother died.

"Diye's Number Nine and Kewambo-Ma, here, is Number Five."

"And there are four more?"

"Yes, four more."

"Ten wives! Imagine! He must be a rich man!" exlaimed the stranger.

"He is," stated Diye.

"And do you love him?"

"Yes, I love him."

"What makes all the women love him?"

"Ha!" snorted her mother-in-law. "I can answer that one. It's because he owns the only love potion from here to the horizon."

Toropo spoke for the first time. "If he owns all this love potion why doesn't he give me some?"

"Don't you love him?" asked the new bride.

"No. And it would make things so much easier if I did."

"You're the odd one for sure," sneered Diye. "Out of the last four wives he married, two of us wanted him before he wanted us."

"But why? Can you tell me why?"

"The powers of the love potion, *ltemo*," put in Rare-Ma.

"Maybe because he is so lovable," answered Diye.

"Impossible," groaned Toropo. "Tell me truthfully, why did you want him?"

"Maybe he was the greatest challenge in sight."

"What was the challenge?" asked Jeep-Ma. "Was it a challenge to make a lecherous old man desire you or was the challenge more in gaining a victory over eight other woman?"

"How was it a victory over you eight women?"

"You know. Making us take a cold back seat while you sat with him right up by the fire."

"Well, one might say it was a challenge all around."

"I think it would be more challenging to make a young man love you," said Toropo. "To be the first woman to awaken love in a young man's heart! Now that would be a challenge. How could it challenge anyone to be a man's tenth love?"

"I don't imagine you had a hard time making the young men love you, did you?" asked the new bride.

Toropo smiled.

"Did you?" asked Jeep-Ma.

"There were a couple interested," answered Toropo, trying to act nonchalant.

"And what happened to them?" Toropo looked into the kind, searching eyes of Keledle-Ma. She felt the older woman was reading her very soul.

"What happened to them if there were some?" prodded Diye.

Toropo turned to her. What a contrast in eyes, she thought. I wonder if Diye's will ever deepen.

"Oh, the main one was just a little too late. Kedle had already told my father that he would give him five more pigs than any other man could offer him."

"*Aminienga glapa*! He must have really wanted you!" exclaimed the bride.

"I suppose so," murmured Toropo studying a little cut on her toe.

When the women reached their hill Toropo turned toward her home.

"May I come along?" asked Keledle-Ma. "*Kapogla*, owiyo, *Ama*." Toropo smiled a welcome.

They sat on opposite sides of the fireplace as Toropo dug out the coals and blew on them. When the fire blazed, she sat in silence while the other woman studied her.

"My soul is bare."

"You are still as unhappy as when you first came?"

"Mm."

"It has been nearly a year now. I hoped you would become reconciled."

"Oh, I am in a way, *Ama*. I realize now there is no hope of any change or release. Perhaps I don't hate Kedle as much as I did."

"You asked why he didn't give you any love potion, daughter. He has."

"Oh, he has?"

"Yes. I myself have put it into your food three different times at his bidding."

"Oh. Then it failed."

"Yes, it failed."

"I'm afraid nothing could ever make me love him, *Ama*. But thank you for trying."

Toropo placed another stick on the fire as the sound of wind and rain enveloped the snug grass hut.

"You love him, don't you, *Ama*?"

"Yes, daughter, I love him."

The older woman traced a pattern in some ashes with the bamboo tongs.

"Doubtless it is much easier for me to love him than for you. I remember him well as a young man."

She scratched out the pattern, smoothed the ashes flat and drew again.

"… as a young man when his bigwig was the biggest bigwig in the whole of the Piamble area." She looked up at Toropo. "His current little wig bothers you, doesn't it?"

"How did you know?" gasped Toropo.

"I see you looking at it like the least you would do is straighten it up … ."

"Or else?"

"Or else tear it off his head?"

"Oh, *Ama*. Truly my soul is bare to you."

"You wouldn't do it though."

"No. Of course not."

"Even though you hate him you would not shame him."

"No."

"I admire you, *nanga bagol*. I wish you were truly my daughter."

"So do I! Then I couldn't be married to Kedle!"

"Oh, Toropo!"

"No. I was just teasing. I appreciate you, *Ama*. You have eased my hard places and soothed my spirit many times. I don't know what I would do here without you."

"The second wife loves you too."

"Yes, I know. I love her also. She is a fine person when you really get to know her, isn't she?"

"Yes, she is. She has surely suffered much. I am sorry now for the way I added to her suffering in the early days. I was so young and selfish and heedless of others' feelings."

"One lives and learns. You have made it up to her the best you can."

"I have tried." Again she smoothed out her ashes.

"What do you hear from your brother?"

"All good news. He likes it at the Teacher's College very much."

"He writes often, doesn't he?"

"Yes. I've had six letters from him in the three months he's been there."

"He seemed like a fine young man."

"He has always been good to me."

"Joe and Janice Holowi are kind too, aren't they?"

"Yes, they are. They have invited me to their home several times lately."

"And the *bagol kondodle* likes you." Toropo studied the older woman quizzically.

"Yes, Tamara and I are good friends"

"How did she happen to come here yesterday? Did she know Kedle was away?"

"Yes, I sent her a note. Toringi took it to her on her way to school."

"Oh, I see. Well, just remember, *nanga bagol kogol*, when you get depressed. There are lots of us who love you. You are not alone."

"Thank you, *Ama*, I'll remember," she promised, smiling brightly.

She adjusted a smoking piece of wood. "Love. That reminds me of something Tamara said. When I told her Rami said she felt God at the mission station that night she nearly died Tamara said, 'She said she felt God? I'm surprised she realized it but she is right. She felt love, and God is love, so she felt God.'"

"Yes, that's true," agreed Keledle-Ma. "The more I learn about God the more I learn to love."

One day not long after Kedle's return, Toringi crawled into Toropo's hut. She sat by the fire looking utterly dejected.

"What's the matter? Did you miss a spelling word?"

"Oh, Toropo!" exclaimed the little girl, burying her face in her knees and bursting into tears. Her whole body began to shake with silent ravaging sobs.

"Why, little Sister!" Toropo moved quickly around the fire to take the young girl in her arms. "What can be the matter?"

No answer but sobs.

"Is your mother all right?"

"Ye-es," Toropo made out, but she could hear no more for the sobbing.

Much later when the crying had exhausted Toringi, she lay still at last with her face buried against Toropo's breast, only an occasional long shuddering sob breaking the stillness.

Toropo laid her lips against Toringi's ear, nuzzled it fondly and whispered, "Can you tell me now, *nanga bagol kogol*?"

It came out in a rush between sobs. "I have to quit school and oh, Toropo, I like it so much! I don't want to quit. I'm at the top of my class, tied with Meku. And last week I beat *him* in New Math and Written Composition. I don't want to quit! I don't want to quit!"

"But why must you quit, little *Konopu*?"

Toringi sat up so quick her head almost bumped Toropo's.

"I'm getting married. Haven't you heard?"

"You're what?"

"I'm getting married."

Toropo looked at her, absolutely stunned. "You can't mean it. You're only a little girl!"

"I know, Toropo. Couldn't you tell *Ara* that for me?"

"Yes, I could. And I will! Believe me!"

"Oh, good! He loves you. He'll listen to you. I do want to go to school so badly."

"Oh, no, *Ango kogol*, don't get your hopes up. Men never listen to women. But yes, I'll talk to him. I'll use all my brains and all my wiles and all my strength and everything I've got, but I don't believe it will do one bit of good."

Toropo thought she could not wait until Kedle came in that evening. Her blood was boiling. She felt like she might explode unless she could talk to him soon.

He came in at dusk. Toropo handed him his *kaukau*. She knew she ought to wait and let him eat first, but she just couldn't hold it in any longer.

"Is it true that you are selling Toringi in marriage?"

"Yes, it's true. Why?"

"How soon is it to take place?" Maybe it was just arrangements being made for future years.

"In a few weeks."

"But she is just a little girl!"

"Oh, not that little."

"Yes, she is! She's far too young for marriage. Why she has no breasts! No breasts at all! She is still as flat-chested as the day her mother weaned her."

"Mm. I know. But living with a man will speed nature up a lot. That's a proven fact, you know. It even did in your own case."

"Yes, I know. But I was almost a woman anyway. Toringi is only a little girl. It's not fair."

"Not fair? Not fair to whom?"

"To Toringi, of course! Who else?"

"Well, I thought maybe you meant it wasn't fair to me or to the man she is to marry."

"I don't follow your thinking, Man! However could it be unfair to you?"

"No need to get excited. Let's just talk it over calmly. I thought you might mean it would be unfair to me if I could not get full price for her, and I was going to assure you that the fellow is paying the full price in spite of her size and youth."

Toropo groaned. She would never learn to think like a man!

"And how could it be unfair to the man who is buying her?"

"Well, obviously, because she is not a woman yet! How will she be able to satisfy him? No breasts, as you said. No hips to speak of, yet. She is as slender, straight and shapeless as a young sapling."

"Well, then I guess it is unfair to the man as well. Why are you selling her to him?"

"Well, I was just going to tell you. It was his own choice. Let me begin from the beginning and explain.

"He is from over on the other side of Marapugul. I don't have any alliances in that area yet and I am happy to establish one now. When I heard he was looking for a girl to be his third wife I invited him to come back with me and look over my daughters. I wasn't expecting him to choose Toringi. Kanambo and Piliembo have both started to mature, you know. But since he asked for Toringi, what difference should that make to me?

"It's his choice.

"I had a daughter once. A full-grown daughter. I lost her just last year, not too long before I married you. I can tell you that made me sick. I had fed her and cared for her all her life only to lose her just when she was old enough to be sold."

"What happened to her?"

"She was drowned in the Cold-Sweet River. She was crossing it with a big *bilum* of *kaukau* on her head when it was in flood stage. The current swept her off her feet and the *kaukau* dragged her down.

"So if a man wants to take a daughter off my hands while she is still little and before any disaster can occur why should I balk? He is paying full price for her as I just said."

"Because it's not fair. That's why you should balk. Because it's not fair to Toringi."

"Why isn't it fair, Woman? For what other purpose is a girl born and raised?"

"Not just for the purpose of satisfying a man! She is born for the same reasons a boy is! To live, and be happy, to love, and enjoy life!"

"Oh, nonsense! Ask the missionaries. Even they say that Adam was created first and Eve was created for him! They will also tell you that Eve was the one who sinned and so she was punished."

He had to stop to cough. "She's not supposed to be happy and enjoy life."

"I thought you were deaf to all that the missionaries say. You only hear what you want to hear. Adam sinned too. Eve's punishment was to bear children in pain.

"Adam's punishment was to till the ground and raise food. You men have it twisted. You make us women do both."

"Ha, ha, ha! Wouldn't I look cute now, out digging *kaukau*! Ha! Ha! I'm afraid God made a mistake that time!"

"But you said ask the *kondodles*. Mr. Talbot is the one who raises their garden. And look at his daughter. He says all the pigs in the world wouldn't be enough to buy her. Why don't you love your daughter like that?"

"Love my daughter? Ah, foolish woman, I only love my wives!"

"Oh, you! You lecherous old man! You don't know what love is!"

"Oh, I don't, don't I?" He reached out for Toropo. She grabbed his fingers and bent them backwards.

"Ouch!" he said, as he raised them to his beard and caressed them.

Looking up at the kunai grass roof he said, "Ten wives and twenty children and she thinks I don't know what love is. What about that?"

"You don't. And don't you dare touch me!" she commanded through gritted teeth. "Don't you touch me again until you tell me you aren't selling Toringi. I'll bite you, kick you, claw you, anything I can do! I hate you, you understand. I hate you! You evil, evil man!"

"Oh, come on, Toropo. Be sensible."

"I am sensible and I tell you, it's not fair to Toringi!"

"But you are being ridiculous. I can't say I won't sell her now after I have already told the man he can have her. How could I do that?"

"You can tell him she doesn't want to be married yet. You can tell him she is just a little girl and she wants to go to school."

"And what would he think of me if I told him my little slip of a daughter didn't want to abide by my wishes?"

"What does it matter what he thinks of you? It ought to matter more to you to treat your own daughter fairly."

"But I told you, stupid woman, that I'm not being unfair to her. I am only giving her a headstart on the fulfilling of the purpose for which she was born and raised."

"And I told you, stupid man, that that isn't the only purpose for which girls are born!"

"And I tell you you're wrong! If you weren't pregnant I'd take a club to you right now. What's more, young woman, you are not going to dictate to me when I can touch you and when I can't. I'll have you when I want you and if you resist I'll beat you, pregnant or not!"

With that he rose and stalked out of the house, as well as a man can stalk when he has to stoop to go through a low doorway. He returned to the manhouse to brood on the stupidity of his youngest wife and the unjustice of her! Why the very idea, thinking she could withhold her body from him! That body he had bought with his own fifteen pigs and five hundred *kina*!

Toropo lay down on her leaf umbrella-mat, praying to God to spare Toringi from a hell-on-earth marriage, and begging Him for wisdom for some better arguments to present to her husband on the little girl's behalf. She was just drifting off to sleep an hour later when she felt a slight movement in her womb. It was as soft and fluttery as the struggles of a butterfly and though she was awake instantly she began to feel, after a minute or two, that she must have imagined it.

Ten minutes later she felt it again. It was a little stronger this time. Her heart exalted. She forgot everything but the new life within her.

"My baby! My child! Part of my bone, my flesh, my blood! What are you my baby, a boy or a girl? She had already asked that question a hundred times, but the baby was more real to her now than it had been before.

She lay there in the darkness imagining its every detail. The soft black ringlets like her own, the large dark eyes, the straight little nose, the sweet little red mouth, the tiny hands and feet! Suddenly Toropo saw her baby in the darkness. "My baby's a girl!" she said aloud. "I know my baby is a girl."

"How can I know it? But I do know it, and I know that I know! I'm as sure of it as that I myself am a female!"

It wasn't an illogical supposition that Kedle's daughter within her was a girl. Eighty percent of his children were girls.

Out of twenty children he had only four sons. So it was logical but it was more than logic. It was more than supposition. Call it woman's intuition. Call it extra-sensory perception. Call it what you will, she knew it was a girl.

Once she accepted her knowledge of its sex, she began to imagine her little daughter's personality. She will be bright, keen, sensitive. She will have a sweet temperament. She will be vibrant, happy. She will love life …. Toropo sat bolt upright in the darkness and spoke aloud, "and she will have nothing but heartbreak all through her life." She groaned aloud.

"Oh God, what am I doing, bringing a child into this wicked world? How can I bring a baby girl into life as Kedle's daughter? Into this land that is so hard on women? I can't. I mustn't ler her live and be born. But how can I stop it? I love her already. My baby. My little girl. My little angel!"

She lay back again on the mat moaning softly. I must not let her be born but how can I kill her? My little daughter. I could not go on living without her now that I have conceived her, now that she is part of me. I could let her be born, and love and cherish her and she would bring me so much happiness that I'd never be sad again. Kedle might buy another wife and leave me alone forever. Marvellous thought. But some day he'd come back and tear my baby from my arms and sell her to some man, maybe even before she has breasts!

Once more a conviction came to her out of the darkness. Again she started and would have sat up, but lay back instead with a groan. I will kill both of us. That is what I'll have to do. It's the only way. The only way! God, is there any other way? Any other way out for my daughter and I? Another way to escape heartache and suffering for her, her whole life long? She lay there silent then, not thinking, only listening in the darkness. But no answer came. God, it's the only way. There is no other way out.

She lay on her mat, planning feverishly, late into the night. At last she fell asleep, emotionally and physically exhausted.

Kedle crept in and fell upon her.

"No fighting. No biting. No clawing, woman! Or I am the one who will bite. I will claw. I'll put a knee in your stomach. Lie still."

Toropo's resolve was strengthened within her. I'll only wait to see if I can help Toringi first.

Chapter Sixteen

Toringi was gone. Sold. Toropo had waited until the end, hoping against hope, but it had all taken place. The man was not old. He was young in fact. He was in the prime of life, strong, handsome, virile. "What could make him want a little girl?" Toropo asked herself. She shuddered.

She found the vine, the *kanda* rope she had prepared and hidden in her garden. She walked slowly to the tree she had chosen, just a short way beyond her garden. Dropping down beneath it, she began hesitantly to fashion the slipknot at one end of the vine.

She found no difficulty in climbing. Her stomach was not yet large enough to hinder her. The tears spilled over and ran down her cheeks as she placed the vine over her head and tied the other end around the limb.

"My baby, my little girl," she whispered. "Move once more for me."

As she crouched in the tree waiting she breathed a prayer. "God forgive me. Forgive me for taking my baby's life and my own. But there is no other way, God. You know all things. Tell me if there is some other way."

"There is a way ..." These were Mr. Talbot's words, reading from the Bible the Sunday before. They floated through her mind. Oh, what was the rest of it?

"There is a way ... that seems right to a man ..."

"What way is that?" Toropo asked. "My way? Suicide?"

There is a way that seems right to a man, but the end of it is the ways of death.

"Yes," thought Toropo, "this is the way of death. The end of this way is death. Do you mean there is another way, God? Is there a way that doesn't end in death?"

The baby moved in her womb as if in answer. Was that stirring, growing life God's answer? There was a power in that tiny movement that made all of Kedle's power seem suddenly old and withered. Would Kedle live forever? Would his power and the power of old men live forever? Or could a new life stir, new men grow up—men like Bani?

Could young men like Bani bring about new laws—laws strong enough to overcome the power of old men to sell their little daughters? Laws strong enough to save her little girl from being sold to a man not of her choice?

Could her daughter be part of a new life like that?

She put her hand to her throat. She felt a pulse of life throb there, like the tiny living movement of her child. Then she felt the rough noose around her warm throat.

Rough like Kedle's gnarled hands.

Suddenly sickened at the thought, she pulled her head out of the noose's embrace.

New life could stir. She was sure of it. But when? And what could she do now? It was the old life that would be waiting for her if she climbed down from the three. She would have to return with her own pulsing life, and the fluttering new life of her child, back to the world of the old men, with their power, their axes and their threats. There was nowhere else to go.

She sat in the tree, thinking, twisting the noose in her hands.

Author's Note

The story of Toropo is based on fact. Every event in the novel also happened in life, to different people at different times. I have turned these events into a fictional story.

I was thirteen years old when I went to live at Piamble at the foot of Mount Giluwe with my parents, who were missionaries. We were the first expatriates to live in that area. My parents built two bush schoolhouses and divided the surrounding children into two groups and began to teach them. Mom took the younger ones; and Dad, the older ones.

"But Mom," I said, "You're leaving out the teenagers! Aren't the teenagers going to have a chance to learn?"

"There are just too many. We can't teach them all."

"I'm thirteen, and I couldn't stand it if I never had the chance to learn any more. And I've already had eight years of school! These teenagers have never even had a chance!"

"Teach them yourself, then, if you want. The school houses are empty in the afternoons."

I asked my fifteen-year-old brother to help me. He taught them numbers and simple maths while I taught them to read and write in their own language, Imbo-Ungu.

Kogla Kereme was an outstanding student in our classes. Once she put on a blouse, only to have it ripped off her by her older brother who was anxious for her bride price. She shared some of her suffering with me. Kogla only lived for a few more years. She was sold in marriage, and died soon after becoming a young mother.

Her younger brother, Philip Kereme, went on from my father's class to Kauapena Community School, Mendi High School and later a university in England.

But it was Kogla who opened my eyes to the plight of Papua New Guinean girls.

Everyone near Piamble knew of Yalo's harem — his collection of wives. He had nine wives when I was thirteen. There had been a tenth one. She had already committed suicide before my arrival. I never knew her.

But I did know the daughter who was swept down the Adleponga River with a heavy bag of *kaukau* on her head. I did know the little daughter of Yala who was sold in marriage before she had any breasts. My mother and I had saved her life in our clinic when she was three years old. And I did help my mother bandage Yalo and three of his wives after a battle like the one depicted in Chapter 12.

I did know the girl at Ialibu who was chopped in two by her husband, directly in front of the military office. She had the most beautiful brown eyes I had ever seen in brown. She was a lovely girl.

Maybe she is Toropo.

I did meet another beautiful bride on Christmas Day, 1969, who came through Katiloma (between Kagua and Erave) in her bridal procession. My fiancé and I were playing a game of badminton that day and our friends called to us to come and see the large cassowary which was part of the bride price. While everyone else looked at the cassowary, I asked, "Who is the husband?" My friends pointed out to me an old, bent, white-bearded man who walked with two canes.

"Who is the bride?" I asked in consternation. My friends pointed out a lovely little ten or twelve-year-old girl poised on the edge of womanhood. I will never forget the one moment our eyes met and locked and I saw into the depths of a very intelligent mind and a sweet personality in a pool clear as crystal.

Maybe she is Toropo.

A few months later when I was on my honeymoon in Port Moresby my mother-in-law wrote to tell me that the little bride had committed suicide by hanging herself. When her husband found her dead, he also hanged himself.

I was twenty-three-years old with many happy years behind me, and a future of happy years stretching out in front of me. But I promised myself I would take enough hours out of my own happiness to write the little bride's story. This little girl had found life so terribly tragic, so stark, that death by hanging had seemed better than life.

I wrote the story finally in 1977, between my adult education classes at Katiloma and my son's first grade classes. Not long after, my husband and I and our three children visited Pila Niningi at Piamble. (Pila's mother, incidentally, is the basis of my portrayal of Toropo's mother.) We learned there that Yalo then had seventeen wives in his harem. Evidently, he still hadn't been able to get that *kondodle* (light-skinned one) who he said was to be his last ...

In 1985, the year my novel was first printed in the magazine *Bikmaus*, three men near Kagua killed their wives within three months. The worst sentence for these crimes was seven months in jail. Papua New Guinea was independent. Village law reigned again, and not even the four-year sentence for wife-killing was being given as when Australian government officers had held court.

The man who cut his wife into many pieces, sending an arm to one village, a foot to another, and so on, had been in the Wiru Valley and had been willing to go to jail for four years in order to teach other young women a lesson.

More recently a young wife, beaten and bleeding, said to a friend, "There's a tree out there, I could take my life that way. Or I could jump off that bank in front of a truck, or I could hire a PMV and ride as far as it could take me ..."

And more recently still, another little wife chose death by overdose.

Toropo is still waiting ... for another way, for a new life.

What shall we do about it?

                            Linda Harvey Kelley
                            August 1992

In the year 2000 I visited Piamble again, and took a photo of Kedle or Yalo Mokoi, with his youngest child, a daughter, born to him and his 25th wife. He had taken fifteen more wives after Toropo, or after my teenage years in Piamble.

I am writing a study guide to go along with this book, and I will do my best to include his photo in it.

In 2008 I returned to PNG again, and was at Pabrabuk when Wane Ninjipa, a Piamble man, and president of Pacific Bible College told me Yalo Mokoi, alias Kedle, had died, but Wane had won him to the Lord before his death.

                            Linda Harvey Kelley
                            January 2009